WINTER IN THRUSH GREEN

WINTER IN THRUSH GREEN

Miss Read

Illustrated by J. S. Goodall

HOUGHTON MIFFLIN COMPANY
Boston • New York

To

Peg and Clare
with love

First Houghton Mifflin paperback edition 2008

www.houghtonmifflinbooks.com

Library of Congress Cataloging-in-Publication Data
Read, Miss
Winter in Thrush Green.
I. Title
PR6069.A42W5 1987 823'.914 87-19456
ISBN 0-89733-264-4

ISBN 978-0-618-88439-1 (pbk.)

Printed in the United States of America

DOC 10 9 8 7 6 5 4 3 2

CONTENTS

PART ONE

The Coming of Winter

PART TWO

Christmas at Thrush Green

PART THREE

The New Year

PART ONE

The Coming of Winter

1. The Newcomer

AUTUMN had come early to Thrush Green. The avenue of horse-chestnuts, which ran across its northerly end, blazed like a bonfire. Every afternoon, as soon as the children at the village school had finished their lessons, they streamed across the wet grass and began to bombard the trees with upthrown sticks as their fathers had done before them. The conkers, glossy as satin, bounced splendidly from their green and white cases and were pounced upon greedily by their young predators.

In the porch of 'The Two Pheasants,' next door to the village school, swung a hanging basket filled with dead geraniums and trails of withered lobelia. All summer through they had enlivened the entrance, but now their bright day was over, and the basket was due to be taken down and stored in the shed at the back of the little inn until summer came again to the Cotswolds.

Chrysanthemums of red and gold glowed on the graves in St Andrew's churchyard, while Mr Piggott the gloomy sexton swept the bright pennies of dead leaves from the paths and cursed fruitlessly as the wind bowled them back again into his newly-swept territory.

The creeper, which climbed over the walls at Doctor Bailey's house and the cottage occupied by two old friends, Ella Bembridge and Dimity Dean, had never flamed so brilliantly as it did this October. The sparkling autumn air, the unusually early frosts and the heavy crop of berries of all sorts made the weather-wise on Thrush Green wag their heads sagely.

'We'll be getting a hard winter this time,' they said in tones of mingled gravity and satisfaction. 'Best get plenty of firing in. Mark my words, it'll be a real winter this one!'

Mr Piggott straightened his aching back, clasped his hands on top of the broom, and surveyed Thrush Green morosely. Behind him lay the bulk of the church, its spire's shadow throwing a neat triangle across the grass. To his right ran the main road from the Cotswold Hills down into the sleepy little market town of Lulling, which Thrush Green adjoined. To his left ran a modest lane which meandered northward to several small villages.

Within fifty yards of him, set along this lane, stood his cottage, next door to 'The Two Pheasants.' The village school, now quiet behind its white palings in the morning sunshine, was next in the row, and beside it was a well-built house of Cotswold stone which stood back from the green. Its front windows stared along the chestnut avenue which joined the two roads. The door was shut, and no smoke plumed skywards from its grey chimneys.

The garden was overgrown and deserted. Dead black roses drooped from the unkempt bushes growing over the face of the house, and the broad flagged path was almost hidden by unswept leaves.

Mr Piggott could see the vegetable garden from his vantage point in the churchyard. A row of bean poles had collapsed, sagging under the weight of the frost-blackened crop. Below the triumphant spires of dock which covered the beds, submerged cabbages, as large as footballs, could be discerned. Onions, left to go to seed, displayed magnificent fluffy heads, and a host of chirruping birds fluttered excitedly about the varied riches of the wilderness.

Mr Piggott clicked his false teeth in disapproval at such

wicked waste, and shook his head at the FOR SALE board which had been erected at the gate the week before.

'Time someone took that over,' he said aloud. 'What's the good weeding this 'ere if all that lot's coming over all the time?' He cast a sour look at the leaves which still danced joyously in his path. Everlasting work! he thought gloomily.

The clock began to whirr above him before striking ten. Mr Piggott's face brightened. Someone came out of 'The Two Pheasants' and latched the door back to the wall hospitably. The faint clinking of glasses could be heard and a snatch of music from the bar's radio set.

Mr Piggott propped his broom against the church railings and set off, with unaccustomed jauntiness, to his haven.

Across the green Ella Bembridge was also looking at the empty house. She had just made her bed, and was busy hanging up her capacious tweed suit in the cupboard, when the sight of a small van drawing up by the FOR SALE board, caught her eye. She folded her sturdy arms upon the window-sill and gazed with interest.

Two men emerged and Ella recognised them. They worked at the local estate agents and lived, she knew, at the village of Nidden a mile or two from Thrush Green. She watched them go inside the gate and start to wrench at the post supporting the board.

'Dim!' called Ella, in a hearty boom, to her companion downstairs. A faint twittering sound came from below.

'Dim!' continued Ella fortissimo, 'they're taking down the board from the corner house! Must be sold!'

Dimity Dean entered the bedroom and joined her friend at the window. A slight, bedraggled figure, clad in an assortment of grey and fawn garments, she was as frail as Ella was robust. She peered short-sightedly at the activity in the distance.

'Isn't that young Edwards? The boy who used to help in the garden?'

'Yes, that's Edwards,' agreed Ella watching the figure heaving at the post.

'Then he's no business to be doing such heavy work!' exclaimed Dimity, much distressed. 'That poor back of his! You know I always wheeled the barrow for him after he slipped that disc.'

'More fool you!' said Ella shortly. 'Bit of exercise will do him good, lazy lout.'

Dimity shook her head mournfully, her eyes filling with sympathetic tears. Of course dear Ella was probably quite right, but Edwards had been such a sweet boy, with an ethereal pale face which quite made one think of Byron. She was relieved to see the board suddenly lurch sideways and the two men carry it out to the van.

'Well,' breathed Dimity, 'I suppose we can look forward to new neighbours now. I do hope they'll fit in at Thrush Green. Quiet people, you know – like us.'

'People who like whooping it up aren't likely to come to Thrush Green,' pointed out Ella, turning her back upon the sunshine. 'Tell you what, we'll see if Winnie Bailey's heard anything when she comes in this morning.'

Dimity clapped a skinny hand to her mouth to stifle a scream.

'Oh, Ella, what a blessing you mentioned her! I'd quite forgotten. I must rush down and get the coffee ready!'

She scuttled down the stairs like a startled hen leaving Ella to speculate upon the future owners of the empty house.

Winnie Bailey was the wife of Doctor Bailey who had been in practice in Lulling and Thrush Green for almost half a century. He still visited a few old patients and occasionally took surgery duty, but since he had retired through ill-health, his young partner Doctor Lovell did more than three-quarters of the work and throve on it.

Life was good to Winnie Bailey. Now that her husband was less busy she found more time for informal visiting, for reading and for the quiet cross-country walks which did so much to refresh her happy spirits.

Thrush Green had changed little since she came first to it as a young wife. True, there were new houses along the lane to Nidden and a large housing estate further west, and in Lulling itself there were twice as many inhabitants. But the triangular green, surrounded by the comfortable Cotswold stone buildings, had altered very little. Winnie Bailey had known those who lived in them, had watched them come and go, grow from children to men and women, and followed their fortunes with an interest which was both shrewd and warm-hearted.

As the wife of a professional man she knew the wisdom of

being discreet. Many came to Winnie Bailey for advice and comfort. They went away knowing full well that their confidences would go no further. In a small community discretion is greatly prized.

She too that morning noticed that the board had gone from the corner house and speculated upon its new owner, as she selected some apples to take to Ella and Dimity who owned no apple trees. She hoped it might be a chess player. Donald, her husband, had so few people to play with these days, and she was no match for him. She picked up a Cox's Orange Pippin and smelt it luxuriously. What a perfect thing it was! She admired its tawny streaks, ranging from palest yellow to glowing amber, which radiated from the satisfying dimple whence its stalk sprang.

She rubbed it lovingly with the white linen cloth, now so old and soft that it crumpled in her hand like tissue paper, and put it carefully in the shallow rush basket among its fellows. Ella would appreciate the picture she was creating, she knew, for beneath Ella's crusty and well-upholstered exterior was a fastidious appreciation of loveliness, which expressed itself in the bold, and sometimes beautiful, designs which she printed for curtains and covers. It was strange, thought Winnie Bailey, that those thick knobbly hands could execute such fine workmanship, while Dimity's frail fingers coped so much more successfully with lighting fires, baking cakes and cleaning the cottage.

The doctor's wife delighted in this incongruous pair. She had known them now for over twenty-five years, and despite their oddities and Ella's brusqueness, was grateful for their unfailing friendship.

She looked at the kitchen clock, which said a quarter to eleven. Donald Bailey was still in bed resting after an unusually busy day. His wife ran up to see him before she set forth with her basket, reflecting as she mounted the stairs on the uncommon devotion of Ella and Dimity.

'I really don't think anything could ever part them,' commented the doctor's wife, addressing the tabby cat who minced past her, *en route* to the kitchen from the Doctor's bed.

But, for once, Winnie Bailey was wrong, as the oncoming winter would show.

'Well, tell us all the news,' said Ella, half an hour later. She leant back in the sagging wicker armchair, which creaked under her weight, raised her coffee cup and prepared to enjoy her old friend's company. 'First of all, how's your husband?'

'Very well really. Rather tired from yesterday. Old Mrs Hoggins wanted him to see a grandchild who is staying with her, and he insisted on going as she's such an old friend, but it rather knocked him up.'

Dimity fluttered between them, proffering first the sugar, then biscuits. From Winnie Bailey she received smiles and thanks; from Ella a fine disregard.

'And what have you heard about the corner house?' queried Dimity, settling at last in her chair, after her moth-like restlessness. 'Who's taken it? Have you heard?'

'Only in a roundabout way from Dotty Harmer,' said Winnie. She stirred her coffee serenely, as though the matter were closed.

Ella snorted, drew out a battered tobacco tin from her pocket and began to roll a very untidy cigarette. The tobacco was villainously black and Mrs Bailey knew from experience that the smoke would be uncommonly pungent. She noticed, with relief, that the window behind her was open.

Ella lit up, drew one or two enormous breaths and expelled the smoke strongly through her nostrils.

'Well, come on,' pressed Ella impatiently. 'What did Dotty say?'

'Nothing actually,' said Winnie, enjoying the situation.

'Then who did?' boomed Ella, jerking her shoulders with exasperation. The coffee cup tilted abruptly and spilled the rest of its contents into Ella's lap.

'Darling,' squeaked Dimity, rising to her feet. 'How dreadful! Let me get a cloth.'

'Don't fuss so, Dim,' snapped her friend, taking out a grubby handkerchief, and wiping the liquid from her lap to the rug with perfunctory sweeps. 'It's your fault, Winnie, for being so perfectly maddening. Do you or do you not know who is coming to the corner house?' She pointed a tobacco-stained forefinger at her guest.

'No,' said Winnie.

Ella threw her handkerchief on the floor with a gesture of despair and frustration. Dimity, anxious to placate her, hastened in where angels would have feared to tread.

'Winnie dear,' she began patiently, 'do you mean "No, you *don't* know" or "No, you *do* know who is coming"?'

'For pity's sake,' roared Ella, 'don't you start, Dim! If Winnie sees fit to drive us insane with her mysteries, well and good. One's enough, in all conscience. For my part, I don't wish to hear who is coming, or not coming, or what Dotty said or did not say, or anything more about the corner house *at all*.'

Exhausted with her tirade she leant back again.

'Any more coffee left?' she asked in a plaintive tone. Dimity hastened forward.

As she filled the cup, Winnie Bailey relented.

'Then I'll just tell Dimity what I've heard, dear, and you need not listen,' she said gently. Ella growled dangerously.

'Betty Bell, who helps Dotty, as you know, has been keeping the corner house aired since the Farmers left, and she has seen most of the people who have looked over it. Three men with families have been, someone from the B.B.C.—'

'Television or sound?' asked Ella eagerly. 'Our television's appalling lately. Everything in a snowstorm or looping the loop. I must say it would be jolly useful to have someone handy to see to it.'

'Oh, not that sort of *useful* person,' exclaimed Winnie, 'just a producer of programmes or an actor, I think.'

'Pity!' said Ella, losing interest.

'Well, who else called?' asked Dimity.

'Several middle-aged women who all found it too large and inconvenient—'

'Which it is,' interrupted Ella. 'D'you remember that ugly great wash-house place at the back? And the corridor and stairs from the kitchen to the dining-room? The soup was always stone cold at Mrs Farmer's parties.'

'And two middle-aged young men, as far as I can gather, who had something to do with ballet,' continued Mrs Bailey, closing her eyes the better to concentrate, 'and then this last man.'

'And what did he do?' pressed Dimity.

'Nothing. I mean he had retired,' said Winnie hastily, as Ella drew a deep breath ready for a second explosion.

'From what?' asked Ella, ominously. 'The army, the navy, the church or the stage?'

'None of them, so Mrs Bell says. I think he's been abroad. Hong Kong or Singapore or Ghana. Maybe it was Borneo or Nigeria, I can't quite recall, but *hot* evidently. He was worried about getting his laundry done daily.'

'Done daily?' boomed Ella.

'Done daily?' quavered Dimity.

'The man must be mental,' said Ella forthrightly, 'if he thinks he's going to get his washing done *daily*. In Thrush Green too. What's wrong with once a week like any other Christian?'

'I don't suppose he really expects to have it done daily *now*,' explained Winnie carefully. 'I imagine that he may have mentioned this matter – the habits of years die hard, you know – and it just stuck in Betty Bell's memory because it seemed so outlandish to her.'

'Seems outlandish to me too,' said Ella. 'When's he coming?'

Mrs Bailey raised limpid eyes to her friend's gaze. She looked mildly surprised.

'I don't know that he is. Betty Bell only told Dotty about the different people who had looked at the house. He was the last, but there may have been more since then. I haven't seen Dotty since last Thursday when I called for my eggs.'

Ella uncrossed her substantial legs, set her brogues firmly on the stained rug and fixed her friend with a fierce glance.

'Winnie Bailey,' she said sternly, 'do you mean to say that you have been going through all this rigmarole – this balderdash – this jiggery-pokery – this leading-up-the-garden – simply to tell us *in the end* that you don't know who is coming to the corner house?'

In the brief silence that followed, the distant cries of children, released from school, floated through the open window. It was twelve o'clock. Winnie Bailey, not a whit abashed, rose to her feet and smiled disarmingly upon her questioner.

'That's right, Ella dear. As I told you at the start, I simply do not know who has taken the corner house. You'll probably know before I do, and I shall expect you to let me hear immediately. There's nothing more maddening,' continued Winnie Bailey serenely, collecting her rush basket from the window-sill, 'than to be kept in suspense.'

'You'd have been burnt for a witch years ago, you hussy,' commented Ella, accompanying her to the door. 'And deserved it!'

2. Wild Surmise

ELLA and Dimity were not the only ones interested in the fate of 'Quetta,' the official name of the empty corner house. Built at the turn of the century for a retired colonel from the Indian army, the house had its name printed on a neat little board which was planted in one of the small lawns which flanked the gates. Apart from young children, who delighted in jumping over it, the name was ignored, and the residence had been known generally for sixty-odd years as 'the corner house.'

The Farmers had lived there for over twenty years and moved only when age and illness overtook them and they were persuaded by a daughter in Somerset to take a small house near her own. Their neighbours on the green missed them, but perhaps the person who mourned their disappearance most wholeheartedly was Paul Young, the eight-year-old son of a local architect who lived in a fine old house which stood beside the chestnut avenue within a stone's throw of the Farmers'.

Ever since he could walk Paul had been free to call at the corner house and, better still, free to roam in the large garden. Old Mr Farmer was a keen naturalist, and finding that the young child was particularly interested in birds and butterflies he encouraged him to watch their activities in his garden and the small copse which adjoined it. Beyond the copse the fields dropped away to a gentle fold of the hills where Dotty Harmer, an eccentric maiden lady much esteemed in Thrush Green and Lulling, had her solitary cottage and flourishing herb garden.

In the distance lay Lulling Woods from whose massed trees many a flight of starlings whirred, or jays called harshly. Paul loved to stand in the little spinney gazing at the fields below or the wooded slope beyond them. His own garden was large, a flat sunny place with trim lawns and bright flower-beds, with here and there a fine old tree which his grandfather had enjoyed. But there was no mystery there. It was all as familiar and everyday as his own pink hands, and although he loved it because it was his home, his growing imagination and delight in secret things made his neighbour's domain far more attractive.

He had said good-bye to the Farmers with much sadness, waving until their car had sunk below sight down the steep hill to Lulling. The sight of Betty Bell closing the gates and returning to the empty house gave him a sense of desolation which he could scarcely endure. He went home dejectedly.

'It's no good fretting, Paul,' his mother said gently, observing his pale face. 'We must hope that the next people will be as nice as the Farmers.'

'It isn't just that,' answered Paul. 'It's the garden, and the birds. There were eleven nests in their copse last spring, and there's red admirals galore on their buddleia. We never get red admirals in our garden.' He kicked morosely at the leg of the kitchen table.

His mother, who was peeling carrots, put one silently before him and watched her sorrowing son find some comfort in its bright crispness. She spoke briskly.

'Well, you know, Paul, you mustn't go into the Farmers' garden now. It's bad luck, but there it is. Perhaps the new owner will let you watch the nests next year, if he sees you don't do any harm. But you mustn't trespass while the house is empty, you understand?'

Paul nodded unhappily. He told himself afterwards that he had not given his word to his mother. He hadn't opened his mouth, he protested to his guilty conscience. Nodding didn't really count, he was to tell himself fiercely many times in the next few weeks.

But Paul was not at ease. For despite his mother's embargo, Paul intended to visit the garden as often as he could. There was more to the Farmers' garden than the red admirals and the birds. There was Chris Mullins.

Christopher Mullins had first burst into Paul's small world in the early summer. At Easter, Paul had left his adored Miss Fogerty who taught him at the village school, and in May began to attend a reliable preparatory school in Lulling.

The new school was much the same size as his earlier one, but to wear a uniform, to carry a satchel, to be taught by masters, and to know that the headmaster was a very great man indeed, impressed Paul considerably.

He knew many of his fellow pupils, for Lulling was a friendly little town and his mother's family and his father's had lived there for many years. In consequence he was not unduly awed, and addressed the bigger boys with less ceremony than some of the newcomers did. When one has shared garden swings, Christmas parties and chicken pox, in a small community, the ice is for ever broken.

But with Christopher Mullins it was different. He had only just arrived from Germany when term began and the attraction of foreign things hung about him. He was bigger, better-looking, older and altogether more interesting than the other boys in Paul's form, and he made it understood that he was only with them because he needed to accustom himself to English methods of education before rising rapidly to the form above – or even the form above that – where he would find his rightful sphere.

Most of the boys treated his superior airs with complete indifference or mild ribaldry, but Paul found them enchanting. He admired Chris's sleek dark hair, his unusually tidy clothes and his superb wrist-watch which had a large red second hand which swept impressively round its shining face. Paul was dazzled by this sophisticated stranger, and the older boy, lacking friendship, was secretly grateful for such homage. When, one day, Paul offered him half his ginger biscuits at morning break, the friendship was sealed and Paul's happiness soared.

Christopher's father was in the army and the family lived in part of an old house on the main road from Lulling to the west. Their garden ran down to the fields near Dotty Harmer's cottage, and it was easy for Christopher to approach Thrush Green from this direction. A path ran through the meadows from Lulling Woods which emerged on to Thrush Green by the side of Mr Piggott's cottage near 'The Two Pheasants.' Sometimes the boy came this way, but more often than not he climbed the grassy hill to the Farmers' copse and there met his jubilant friend.

They had kept their meetings secret, partly because Chris was trespassing, but largely because it made the whole affair deliciously exciting. Between the spinney and the herbaceous border was a thick growth of ox-eyed daisies which formed a background for the lower-growing plants. Here, in this hidden greenness, the two boys had made their headquarters. There was nothing to show that it was a place of any importance, only two small chalked letters on a tree trunk – a C and a P side by side – which would escape the Farmers' old eyes or the occasional glance of Mr Piggott when he 'obliged' two or three times a year.

Their activities were innocent enough. They exchanged news of nests, animals, friends or relatives, in that order of importance. Sometimes they sat amicably in the damp green hide-out and ate liquorice boot-laces or a fearsomely sticky hardbake which was sold in one of the back streets of Lulling and was much prized for its staying qualities. Once they smoked a cigarette which Paul had brought from home, but they did not repeat that experiment.

They met in all that summer about six times, and the place had grown very dear to young Paul. At school, before the other boys, they said nothing about their secret meetings. It was this delicious intimacy which Paul mourned on the departure of the Farmers.

With the coming of autumn the meetings had become less frequent. Not only was it too cold to sit crouched in the green gloom behind the daisies, but the frosts had thinned them sadly, so that small boys might be observed far too easily. They decided that in future they must shift their headquarters to the spinney itself where there was more cover.

And Paul, rebelliously crunching his carrot, was determined to keep his trysts with Chris Mullins despite his mother's words and the uncomfortable stirrings of his own conscience.

After the removal of the signboard early in October, the inhabitants of Thrush Green renewed their energies and attacked the autumn jobs that pressed upon them. The air was exhilarating, the sun shone with that peculiar brilliance which is only seen in a clear October sky, and the autumn leaves added to the bright glory.

Apples were being picked, potatoes dug, and herbaceous borders tidied, and Sam Curdle's ancient lorry creaked and shuddered under the loads of wood which it bore down the lane from Nidden to prudent householders who were filling up their store sheds against the winter's cold.

Sam Curdle lived in a caravan a mile or two from Thrush Green and eked out a living from various types of piece-work for local farmers, by selling logs or acting as carrier in the district. For over two years now he had supported himself and his wife Bella and their three children in this way, and he was now part of Thrush Green's life; but the good people of that place remembered his dismissal from the great Mrs Curdle's Fair, on the last May Day that that amazing old lady had seen, and were careful not to trust Sam with anything of particular value. Mrs Curdle had found that he was a thief. Thrush Green, who had known Mrs Curdle for over fifty years, knew that she was usually right, and did not forget.

It was noticed, too, that Mrs Curdle's grave which lay in St Andrew's churchyard, at her own request, was never visited by Sam or his family, and though this was understandable when one remembered the nature of their parting, yet it was not easily forgiven. As the landlord of 'The Two Pheasants' was heard to say:

' 'Tain't right that the only relative living near should neglect the old lady like that – never mind what passed between them! If young Ben weren't away with the Fair he'd keep it fit for a queen, that I don't doubt. A proper mean-spirited fellow that Sam. I don't trust him no further than I can see him!' And that expressed, pretty correctly, the feelings of the rest of Thrush Green.

Nevertheless, he had to be lived with and he seemed willing to make a useful contribution to village life, so that people spoke civilly to Sam, gave him their custom and odd jobs to do, and kept their misgivings to themselves.

One bright October afternoon Winnie Bailey had engaged Sam to sweep up dead leaves and make a bonfire, which he did with much energy. The blue smoke spiralled skywards filling the air with that sad scent which is the essence of autumn.

Winnie Bailey hoed vigorously round the rose bushes in the front garden which looked upon Thrush Green. From Joan

Young's garden she could hear the sound of a lawn mower doing its final work before the grass grew too long and wet. In the playground of the village school Miss Fogerty was taking games with the youngest children, and their thin voices could be heard piping like winter robins' as they played the ancient singing games.

The doctor was having an afternoon nap and Mrs Bailey was intent on finishing the rose-beds before tea-time. Her hair had escaped from its pins, her face glowed with fresh air and exercise, and she was just congratulating herself upon her progress, when Ella's hearty voice boomed from the gate.

'Can you do with some sweet williams?'

Winnie Bailey propped the hoe against the wall and went to greet her.

'Come in, Ella.'

'Can't stop, my dear. I'm off to get Sam Curdle to leave us some wood.'

'He's here, this minute, in the garden,' said Winnie. 'So you'd better come in and save yourself a trip.'

Ella thrust an untidy bundle of plants wrapped in newspaper into Winnie Bailey's arms, and opened the gate.

'They're wonderful,' said Mrs Bailey with genuine enthusiasm. 'I'll put them in as soon as I've finished hoeing. Sam's at the back, if you'd like a word with him.'

Ella stumped resolutely out of sight. Voices could be heard above the scratching of Winnie's renewed hoeing, but within five minutes Ella returned.

'That's done. Good thing I looked in. Ever had any wood from Sam? Does he give you a square deal? Always was such a blighted twister, it makes you wonder.'

Winnie Bailey thought, not for the first time, that it was amazing how well Ella's voice carried, and wished that if she could not moderate her tones she would at least refrain from putting her opinions into such forceful language. She had no doubt that Sam had heard every syllable.

'As a matter of fact I had a load of logs from him last year, and they were very good indeed,' answered Mrs Bailey in a low voice, hoping in vain that Ella would take the hint. 'I didn't mention it to Donald, for he abominates the fellow, as you know, after the way he treated old Mrs Curdle, so say nothing if it ever crops up.'

'Trust me!' shouted Ella cheerfully.

She made her way to the gate, paused with one massive hand on the post, and nodded across to the corner house.

'Any more news?'

'None, as far as I know,' confessed Mrs Bailey.

'I did my best at Johnsons' cocktail party last week,' said Ella. 'Got young Pennefather in a corner and asked him outright, but you know what these estate agents are. Came over all pursed-lips and prissy about professional duties to his client!'

'Well—' began Winnie diffidently.

'Lot of tomfoolery!' said Ella belligerently, sweeping aside the interruption. 'Anyone'd think he'd had to take the hypocrite's oath or whatever that mumbo-jumbo is that doctors have to swear. I told him flat – "Look here, my boy, don't you come the dedicated professional over me. I remember you kicking in your pram, and you don't impress me any more now than you did then!" Stuffy young ass!'

Ella snorted with indignation, and Winnie Bailey was hard put to it to hide her laughter.

'Relax, Ella. We're bound to know before long, and I should hate to have to wake poor Donald up to attend to an apoplectic fit in the front garden.'

Ella's glare subsided somewhat and was replaced by a smile as she wrenched open the gate.

'Don't think it will come to that yet,' said she, and set off with martial strides to her own house.

Half an hour later Mrs Bailey made her way across the green to St Andrew's church with the last of the roses in her basket. It was her turn to arrange the flowers on the altar and she wanted to get them done before the daylight faded.

Mr Piggott was trimming the edges of the grass paths with a pair of shears. He knelt on a folded sack which he shifted along, bit by bit, as the slow work progressed.

Mrs Bailey went over to speak to him, and the sexton rose painfully to his feet, sighing heavily.

'Anything you want?' he asked with a martyred air.

'Nothing at all, Mr Piggott,' said Winnie cheerfully, 'except to ask how you are.'

'Too busy,' grunted the sexton. 'Too busy by half! All these 'ere edges to clip and more graves to keep tidy than I ought to be asked to do. Look at old lady Curdle's there! What's to stop Sam keeping the grass trimmed? My girl's husband Ben won't half be wild if he finds his old gran's grave neglected, but there's too much here for one pair of hands.'

Winnie Bailey stepped across to the turfed mound against the churchyard wall. A neat stone at its head said simply:

ANNIE CURDLE
1878–1959

The little stone flower vase at its foot was empty except for a little rainwater which had collected there. Mrs Bailey selected half a dozen roses from her basket and put them in one by one, thinking as she did so of the dozens of bunches of flowers she had received from the old lady during her lifetime.

Mr Piggott watched in morose silence, scraping the mud

from his boots on a convenient tussock of coarse grass. He steadied himself by resting his weight on a mossy old tombstone. The inscription was almost obliterated by the passage of years and the grey lichen which was creeping inexorably across the face.

'Ah, we've got all sorts here,' commented Mr Piggott with lugubrious levity. 'They say this chap was shipped back from Africa in a barrel of rum.' He patted the tombstone kindly, and his face brightened at the thought.

'I can't believe that,' expostulated Mrs Bailey, coming round the stone to peer at the inscription. 'Oh no, Piggott! This is Nathaniel Patten's grave. I'm sure he'd never have anything to do with rum. He was a strict teetotaller and a wonderful missionary, I believe.'

'Maybe he was,' said old Piggott stoutly, 'but in them days bodies was brought home from foreign parts in spirits. That I do know. I'll lay a wager old Nathaniel here ended up in rum, even if he didn't hold with it during his lifetime.'

'I must ask the doctor about it, if I can remember,' replied Mrs Bailey, picking up her basket and making her way towards the church. 'And I really must find out more about Nathaniel Patten one day.'

As she entered the quiet church intent upon her duties, she little thought that Nathaniel Patten, born so long ago in Thrush Green and now lying so still beneath his grassy coverlet, would be the cause of so much consternation to his birthplace.

3. Miss Fogerty Rises to the Occasion

ONE Monday morning in October Miss Fogerty arrived at the village school on Thrush Green at her usual time of twenty to nine.

Her headmistress, Miss Watson, took prayers with the forty-odd pupils at nine o'clock sharp, and Miss Fogerty, who took the infants' class and was the only other teacher at the establishment, liked to have a few minutes to put out her register and inkstand, unlock the cupboards and her desk drawer, check that the caretaker had filled the coal scuttle and left a clean duster, and to be ready for any early arrivals with bunches of flowers which might need vases of water for their refreshment.

She had enjoyed her ten-minute walk from lodgings on the main road. The air was crisp, the sun coming up strongly behind the trees on Thrush Green. Zealous housewives, who had prudently put their washing to soak on Sunday night, were already busy pegging it out and congratulating themselves upon the fine weather. Miss Fogerty, whose circumstances obliged her to do her own washing on Saturday morning each week, was glad to see their industry rewarded. Unless one was prepared to get one's washing out *really early* in October, she told herself, as she trotted along briskly, then one might as well dry it by the fire, for the days were so short that it virtually didn't dry at all after three or four in the afternoon. Unless, of course, a gale blew up, and that did more harm than good to clothes, winding them round the line and wrenching the material. Why, only on Saturday, her best pair of plated lisle stockings had been sorely twisted round the washing line and she greatly feared the fibres had been damaged.

With such matters had earnest little Miss Fogerty busied herself as she hurried along. There were very few children about, and when she reached the school only half a dozen or so were at large in the playground. Punctuality was not a strong point at Thrush Green, and Miss Watson's insistence on prayers at nine sharp was one of her methods of correction. Late-comers were not allowed in, and were obliged to wait in the draughty lobby. While their more time-conscious brethren received spiritual refreshment for the day, Miss Watson hoped that they would meditate upon their own shortcomings. In fact, the malefactors usually ate sweets, redistributed the hats and coats of the pious, for their future annoyance, among the coat-pegs, and played marbles. They were wise enough to choose a large rubber mat by the door for this purpose, for experience had shown them that the uneven brick floor made a noisy, as well as unpredictable, playing ground, and Miss Fogerty had been known to slip out during the reading of the Bible passage to see what all the rumbling was about. Hardened late-comers were prudent enough to play marbles only while the piano tinkled out the morning hymn, for then Miss Fogerty, they knew, would be at the keyboard and Miss Watson leading the children's singing. After that it was as well to compose their faces into expressions of humility and regret, and to hope secretly that they would be let off with a caution, as the congregation returned to its studies.

The school was empty when Miss Fogerty clattered her way over the door-scraper to her room. That did not surprise her, for Miss Watson lived at the school house next door, and might be busy with her last-minute chores. She usually arrived about a quarter to nine, greeted her colleague, read her correspondence and was then prepared to face the assembled school.

Miss Fogerty hung up her tweed coat and her brown felt hat behind the classroom door, and set about unlocking the cupboards. There were little tatters of paper at the bottom of the one by the fireplace, where the raffia and other handwork materials were kept and Miss Fogerty looked at them with alarm and suspicion. She had thought for some time that a mouse lived there. She must remember to tell Mrs Cooke to set a trap. Mice were one of the few things that Miss Fogerty could not endure. It would be dreadful if one ran out while the children were present and she made an exhibition of herself by screaming! After surveying the jungle of cane, raffia and cardboard which rioted gloriously together, and which could well offer a dozen comfortable homes to abundant mice families, Miss Fogerty firmly shut the door and relocked it. The children should have crayons and drawing paper this afternoon from the cupboard on the far side of the room, she decided. Mrs Cooke must deal with this crisis before she approached the handwork cupboard again.

The clock stood at five to nine, and now the cries and shouts of two or three dozen children could be heard. Miss Fogerty made her way to the only other classroom, and stopped short on the threshold with surprise. It was empty.

Miss Fogerty noted the clean duster folded neatly in the very centre of Miss Watson's desk, the tidy rows of tables and chairs awaiting their occupants, and the large reproduction of Holman Hunt's 'The Light of the World' in whose dusky glass Miss Fogerty could see her own figure reflected.

What should she do? Could Miss Watson have overslept? Could she be ill? Either possibility seemed difficult to believe. In the twelve years since Miss Watson's coming she had neither overslept nor had a day's indisposition. It would be very awkward if she called at the house and Miss Watson were just about to come over. It would look *officious*, poor Miss Fogerty told herself, and that could not be borne. Miss Fogerty was a little afraid of Miss Watson, for though she herself had spent thirty years at Thrush Green School, she was only the assistant teacher and she had been taught to respect her betters. And

Miss Watson, of course, really was her better, for she had been a headmistress before this, and had taught in town schools, so large and magnificent, that naturally she was much wiser and more experienced. She was consistently kind to faded little Miss Fogerty and very willing to show her new methods of threading beads and making plasticine crumpets, explaining patiently, as she did so, the psychological implications behind these activities in words of three or, more often, four syllables. Miss Fogerty was humbly grateful for her goodwill, but would never have dreamt of imposing upon it. Miss Fogerty knew her place.

While she hovered on the threshold, patting her wispy hair into place with an agitated hand and looking distractedly at her reflection in 'The Light of the World,' a breathless child hurried into the lobby, calling her name.

'Miss Fogerty! Miss Fogerty!'

He rushed towards her so violently that Miss Fogerty put out her hands to grasp his shoulders before he should butt her to the ground.

The child looked up at her, wide-eyed. He looked awe-stricken.

'Miss Watson called me up to her window, miss, and says you're to go over there.'

'Very well,' said Miss Fogerty, calmly. 'There's no need to get so excited. Take off your coat and hang it up. You can go to your room now.'

The child continued to gaze at her.

'But, miss,' he blurted out, 'Miss Watson – she – she's still in her nightdress and the clock's struck nine.'

Miss Watson's appearance when she opened the side door alarmed Miss Fogerty quite as much as it had the small boy.

Her nightdress was decently covered by a red dressing-gown,

but her face was drawn with pain and she swayed dizzily against the door jamb.

'What has happened?' exclaimed Miss Fogerty, entering the house.

Miss Watson closed the door and leant heavily against it.

'I've been attacked – hit on the head,' said Miss Watson. She sounded dazed and vaguely surprised. A hand went fumbling among her untidy grey locks and Miss Fogerty, much shocked, put her hand under her headmistress's elbow to steady her.

'Come and sit down. I'll ring Doctor Lovell. He'll be at home now. Tell me what happened.'

'I can't walk,' answered Miss Watson, leaning on Miss Fogerty's frail shoulder. 'I seem to have sprained my ankle as I fell. It is most painful.'

She held out a bare leg, and certainly the ankle was misshapen and much swollen. Purplish patches were already forming and Miss Fogerty knew from her first-aid classes that she should really be applying hot and cold water in turn to the damaged joint. But could poor Miss Watson, in her present state of shock, stand such treatment? She helped the younger woman to the kitchen, put her on a chair and looked round for the kettle.

'There's nothing like a cup of tea, dear,' she said comfortingly, as she filled it. 'With plenty of sugar.'

Miss Watson shuddered but made no reply. Her assistant switched on the kettle and surveyed her headmistress anxiously. Her usual feeling of respect, mingled with a little fear, had been replaced by the warmest concern. For the first time in their acquaintanceship Miss Fogerty was in charge.

'The door-bell rang about half-past five, I suppose,' began Miss Watson hesitantly. 'It was still dark. I leant out of the bedroom window and there was a man waiting there who said there had been a car crash and could he telephone.'

'What did he look like?' asked Miss Fogerty.

'I couldn't see. I said I'd come down. I put on my dressing-gown and slippers and opened the front door—' She broke off suddenly, and took a deep breath. Miss Fogerty was smitten by the look of horror on her headmistress's face.

'Don't tell me, my dear, if it upsets you. There's really no need.' She patted the red dressing-gown soothingly, but Miss Watson pulled herself together and continued.

'He'd tied a black scarf, or a stocking, or something over his face, and I could only see his eyes between that and his hat brim. He had a thick stick of some kind – quite short – in his hand, and he said something about this being a hold-up, or a stick-up or some term I really didn't understand. I bent forward to see if I could recognise him – there was something vaguely familiar about him, the voice perhaps – and then he hit me on the side of my head—' Poor Miss Watson faltered and her eyes filled with tears at the memory of that vicious blow.

The kettle's lid began rattling merrily and Miss Fogerty, clucking sympathetically, began to make the tea.

'I seem to remember him pushing past me. I'd crumpled on to the door mat and I remember a fearful pain, but whether it was my head or my ankle, I don't really know. When I came round again the door was shut and he'd vanished. It was beginning to get light then.'

'Why didn't you get help before?' asked Miss Fogerty. 'It must have been about seven o'clock then. He will have got clear by now.'

'I was so terribly sick,' confessed Miss Watson. 'I managed to crawl to the outside lavatory and I've been there most of the time.'

'You poor, poor dear,' cried Miss Fogerty. 'And you must be so cold, too!'

'I couldn't manage the stairs, otherwise I should have got

dressed. But I thought I would wait until I heard you arrive, and then I knew I should be all right.'

Miss Fogerty glowed with pleasure. It was not often, in her timid life, that she had been wanted. To know that she was needed by someone gave her a heady sense of power. She poured out the tea with care and put the cup carefully before her patient.

'Shall I lift it for you?' she asked solicitously, but Miss Watson shook her head, raising the steaming cup herself and sipped gratefully.

'The children—' she said suddenly, as their exuberant voices penetrated the quietness of the kitchen.

'Don't worry,' said Miss Fogerty with newly-found authority. 'I'll just speak to the bigger ones, then I'll be back to ring the doctor.'

'Don't tell them anything about this,' begged Miss Watson

with sudden agitation. 'You know what Thrush Green is. It will be all round the place in no time.'

Miss Fogerty assured her that nothing would be disclosed and slipped out of the side door.

The children were shouting and playing, revelling in this unexpected addition to their pre-school games time.

Miss Fogerty leant over the low dry-stone wall which separated the playground from the school-house garden. She beckoned to two of the bigger girls.

'Keep an eye on the young ones, my dears. I'll be with you in a minute, then we'll all go in.'

'Is Miss Watson ill?' asked one, her eyes alight with pleasurable anticipation.

Miss Fogerty was torn between telling the truth and the remembrance of her promise to her headmistress. She temporised wisely.

'Not really dear, but she won't be over for a little while. There's nothing for you to worry about.'

She hastened back to her duties.

Her patient had finished her tea and now leant back with her eyes closed and the swollen ankle propped up on another chair. She opened her eyes as Miss Fogerty approached, and smiled faintly.

'Tell me,' said Miss Fogerty, who had just remembered something. 'Did the man take anything?'

'He took the purse from my bag. There wasn't much in it, and my wallet, with about six pounds, I believe.'

Miss Fogerty was profoundly shocked. Six pounds was a lot of money for a schoolteacher to lose even if she were a headmistress.

'And I think he may have found my jewel box upstairs, but of course I haven't been up there to see. It hadn't much of value in it, except to me, I mean. There was a string of seed pearls my father gave me, and two rings of my mother's and a brooch or two – but nothing worth a lot of money.'

'We must ring the police as well as Doctor Lovell,' exclaimed Miss Fogerty.

'Must we?' cried Miss Watson, her face puckering. 'Oh dear, I do hate all this fuss – but I suppose it is our duty.'

Miss Fogerty's heart smote her at the sight of her patient's distress. It reminded her too that she should really get her into bed so that she could recover a little from the shocks she had received. She sprang to her feet, with new-found strength, and went to help her headmistress.

'Back to bed for you,' she said firmly, 'and then I'm going to the telephone. Up you come!'

Five minutes later, with her patient safely tucked up, Miss Fogerty spoke to Doctor Lovell and then to Lulling Police Station. That done, she went over to the school playground to face the forty or more children for whom she alone would be responsible that day.

Normally the thought would have made timid little Miss Fogerty quail. But today, fortified by her experiences, feeling six feet high and a tower of strength, Miss Fogerty led the entire school into morning assembly and faced a host of questioning eyes with unaccustomed composure and authority.

For the first time in her life Miss Fogerty was in command, and found she liked it.

As Miss Watson had feared, the word had flown round Thrush Green with exceptional rapidity. It was too much to hope that the visit of Doctor Lovell, and later, the sight of a policeman walking up the path to the school-house, should pass unnoticed, on a fine Monday morning, in Thrush Green. Neighbours shaking mats, pegging out the week's washing or simply gossiping over the hedges, saw the signs and spread the tales.

'Probably got a touch of this 'ere flu that's going round,' said one, as Doctor Lovell strode briskly towards the school-house door. 'It's gastrical this year,' she added, airing her medical knowledge.

'Hasn't looked well for weeks,' said another. 'Very tiring life, that teaching. Everlasting bawling at the kids – must knock you up in the end.'

'Poor Miss Watson, wonder what ails her? At a funny age, of course, for a spinster,' commented a third matron, taking a swipe at her screaming ninth and youngest, and feeling unaccountably superior at the same time.

Within ten minutes of Doctor Lovell's appearance Thrush Green had burdened Miss Watson with every ill from ear-ache to epilepsy, and felt for her an all-embracing sympathy.

Within half an hour the policeman arrived. He was hot and breathless, having pushed his bicycle up the steep hill from Lulling. He vanished inside the house and the temperature rose again on Thrush Green.

'If it weren't that Doctor Lovell's so very particular I'd say she'd been assaulted,' said one neighbour earnestly to another, damning in one breath the morals of the rest of the medical profession and Miss Watson's modest charms.

'Could be attempted suicide,' said another, her eye brightening. 'Teaching's enough to turn your head at times. You can't wonder with children round you all day.'

'That's true,' agreed her crony, nodding her head sagely. 'Poor Miss Watson's probably come over violent and Doctor's sent for the police. Unless, of course, she's done something real bad and just confessed it to the doctor—'

The tongues wagged gaily. By the time the children came out to play at ten-thirty Thrush Green had Miss Watson convicted of every crime from forgetting to renew her television licence – this was the most charitable suggestion – to slitting young Doctor Lovell's throat with the bread-knife whilst in the grip of a violent brainstorm brought on by twelve years' non-stop teaching. This was the opinion of those who allowed their thoughts to be coloured by the recent reading of their Sunday newspapers. There was certainly enough to keep Thrush Green pleasurably amused for many happy days, and by the time Doctor Lovell had departed, and the policeman had stowed away his pocket-book with poor Miss Watson's statement in it and a detailed description of the missing purse, wallet – and, alas – the jewel case and a small gilt alarm clock, there were enough rumours flying round the green to last a year.

As Ella Bembridge said afterwards: 'It never rains but it pours,' for before the children returned to school at ten forty-five prompt, another momentous happening shook Thrush Green.

A large Daimler car glided to the gate of the corner house. Out stepped a tall military figure who stood looking about him, just long enough for the watchful eyes of his future neighbours to notice his sunburnt face and white moustache, before taking out a door-key, hurrying up the path and letting himself into his new home.

For a brief moment Miss Watson's blaze of glory was extinguished in the dazzling light of this new event.

At last, the corner house was occupied.

4. Plans for a Party

SOME days after this excitement, Ella and Dimity sat at the dining-room table writing invitations. It would be more truthful to say that Dimity was doing the writing, while Ella conned a list and occasionally thumped a stamp on the addressed envelopes.

'About time we did this,' commented Ella, watching Dimity's careful pen inscribing SHERRY in the left-hand corner. 'How long since we gave a blow-out, Dim?'

'Quite two years,' said Dimity, selecting an envelope. 'I know it was in the summer, soon after Mrs Curdle's fair came. The last time we saw her,' added Dimity, her eyes beginning to look misty.

Ella stirred herself to be bracing. Much too sympathetic, poor old Dim! Ought to have had a husband and six children to lavish all that affection on, thought Ella, not for the first time.

'Grand old girl,' agreed Ella heartily. 'Well, she had a good run for her money, you know, and the fair's still going strong under young Ben. I hear he's coming to Thrush Green for Christmas with Molly, to see old Piggott.'

As she had intended, this diverted Dimity's attention.

'That will be nice. I'd like to see Molly Piggott again – Curdle, I mean.' Dimity smiled at the thought and attacked the stack of cards again.

'Who have we done now?' she asked Ella, who was ticking the list.

'The Baileys, the Youngs, the rector, the Lovells, Dotty, and the three Lovelock sisters. Only four more to do. I can't see where we're going to put them anyway in this cottage.'

'People shrink at cocktail parties,' Dimity assured her. 'It's because they stand up and are packed together neatly. At tea parties their legs are spread all over the floor.'

'Awful lot of women,' mourned Ella surveying the list.

'I wouldn't say they're awful,' said Dimity, sounding shocked.

'No, no,' replied Ella testily. 'They're *not* awful. There's just too many of them.' Her face brightened.

'Dim, we've forgotten to put down the new man. Write one quickly.'

'But we don't know him,' objected Dimity. 'We haven't called yet.'

'I have,' said Ella briefly. Dimity looked at her with her mouth open.

'You didn't tell me.'

'I forgot. I took the parish magazine in and he was in the front garden. Seems a nice man.'

Dimity looked a little affronted, but obediently inscribed a card and put it in an envelope. She looked up, pen hovering.

'What is he called?'

'Harold Shoosmith,' said Ella promptly. 'With an "o" instead of "e" in "Shoo." And an "o" for Harold, I'm glad to say, not "a." If there's one thing I can't abide it's a Harald with an "a." Like "Hark the Harald Angels Sing," ' added Ella facetiously.

Dimity's pen remained poised in mid-air. She ignored Ella's weak joke with unaccustomed severity.

'Is he retired army or navy?' she asked.

'Search me,' said Ella. 'Winnie Bailey says he's a Lieutenant-Commander, Joan Young says he's a Major, and Ruth Lovell heard he was a Squadron-Leader. As far as Thrush Green's concerned after a week's acquaintanceship I should say "Esq." would fit the case perfectly.'

She watched Dimity write the address and sighed happily as it was pushed over to her to stamp.

'I must say it's a real pleasure to have an unattached man at one of our parties. Can't remember the last time we had one under our roof, can you, Dim?'

'The rector comes often enough,' pointed out Dimity, a little tartly.

'Well, you can't count the rector,' said Ella reasonably, 'poppet though he is. Besides, he's a widower.'

'So may Harold Shoosmith be,' said Dimity, writing rather fast. Her mouth was pursed, and Ella could see that she had not been completely forgiven for having met the newcomer before her friend. She watched the hurrying pen with mingled guilt and amusement.

Dimity completed the card and looked across at Ella meaningly.

'Or even married!' she said with emphasis.

And she might just as well have added 'So there!' thought Ella, stamping the envelope in silence, from the hint of triumph in her voice.

Ella's lively interest in Harold Shoosmith was shared by the rest of Thrush Green. It was said that he was retired from the army, the navy, the air force, the civil service and the B.B.C. He had been a tea-planter in Ceylon, a cocoa-adviser in Ghana, and a coffee-blender in Brazil. It also appeared that he had owned a sugar plantation in Jamaica, a rubber plantation in Malaya and a diamond mine – quite a small one, actually, but with exceptionally fine diamonds – in South Africa.

Thrush Green was sorry to hear that he had never been married, had been married unhappily and was now separated from his wife, had been happily married and lost his wife in childbirth and (disastrously), still married, with a wife who would be coming to live with him at the corner house within a few days.

The inhabitants of Thrush Green were able to gaze their fill at the stranger on the first Sunday after his arrival, as he attended morning service in a dove-grey suit which was far better cut, everyone agreed, than those of the other males in the congregation. The rector and one or two other neighbours had called upon him already and pronounced him 'a very nice man' or 'a decent sort of fellow' according to sex.

To the rector's unfeigned delight the newcomer was among the very few communicants at the altar rail at the eight o'clock service on the following Sunday. About half a dozen faithful female Christians kept the rector company at early service usually, and these included Dimity Dean – but not Ella who went to church less frequently – and Dotty Harmer. It did the rector's heart good to see a man among his small flock, and he hoped that others might follow his example.

Betty Bell was the chief informant about Harold Shoosmith for she had been engaged for three mornings and three evenings a week. The morning engagements Thrush Green could readily understand, for a man living alone could not be expected to polish and clean, to cook and scrub, and to wash and iron for himself; though, as Ella pointed out, plenty of women lived alone and did all that with one hand tied behind them, and often went out to work as well into the bargain, and no one considered it remarkable.

The evening engagements were readily explained by Betty Bell herself. She went for an hour and a half to give him a hot cooked dinner, which she had prepared in the morning, and to wash-up afterwards.

'He's a very clever kind of man,' said Betty to her other employer, Dotty Harmer, one morning. 'He wants to learn to cook for himself. Being out in those hot countries, you know, he's never had a chance to learn. The kitchen's full of black people falling over themselves to do the work, and he's never been allowed to see his own dinner cooking, so I hear.'

'I should have thought he could have managed a fried egg,' said Dotty cutting up quinces at the table. 'Ah, Betty,' she sighed sadly, peering up at the girl through her thick glasses, 'this means the real end of summer, you know. When I make quince jam I know it's the last of the season. It'll soon be November, Betty, and winter will be here.'

'That's what I told Mr Shoosmith,' agreed Betty, returning to her present consuming interest. ' "You want to know how to cook a meal for yourself, in case I can't get here one winter's day," I said to him. So I've shown him how to fry bacon and egg and sausage, and how to make a stew. He's real quick at picking things up, I must say.'

'Poor man,' said Dotty, 'he'll miss the sun, I dare say. Would you like to take him a pot of my jam when it's done?' Her face brightened at the thought. She had introduced herself to the newcomer after early morning service and had been glad to welcome such an attractive addition to the Thrush Green circle.

Betty accepted the offer guardedly and made a mental note to warn the unsuspecting recipient against eating it. Dotty, as a keen herbalist and dietician, could never refrain from adding a few sprigs of this, and a drop or two of that, to her dishes in order to give them added vitamin content, and the number of people who had been attacked with 'Dotty's Collywobbles,' as a result of her cooking, was prodigious.

At that moment the postman appeared at the kitchen window and handed in an untidy parcel and one letter.

'This must be my dried coltsfoot and the other things for my winter ointments and cough cures,' said Dotty excitedly, dropping the quinces and tearing at the parcel with sticky fingers. Some strongly-smelling dead foliage fell upon the kitchen table and the black cat who was sunning herself upon it near the jam-making operations. Outraged, she leapt down and stalked towards the stove, tail quivering erect with indignation.

'There now,' said Betty, 'you've been and upset Mrs Curdle; and her expecting too.'

Dotty was now reading the card which she had extracted from the envelope. The scattered herbs lay unheeded where they had fallen.

'Oh, how lovely!' exclaimed Dotty, her wrinkled face alight with pleasure. 'Miss Bembridge and Miss Dean are giving a sherry party on October 31st. Now, isn't that nice?'

'All Hallows E'en,' commented Betty, bending to stroke Mrs Curdle's ruffled dignity. She had been named after the famous old lady because she had been born on the day that Curdle's Fair visited Thrush Green over two years before. The cat shared with her famous namesake some of her dark magnificence and queenly dominance. She now allowed Betty to smooth her fur, but turned her back upon her thoughtless mistress.

'So it is,' cried Dotty. 'A party on All Hallows E'en! Well, well, I must certainly go to that!'

She picked up some of the quinces, together with a few stray herbs from the parcel, and dropped them into a saucepan.

As she stirred she peered closely into the bubbling brew, and Mrs Curdle, suspecting that food might be forthcoming, deigned to return to her mistress's side.

'Proper witches' party it will be, and no mistake,' thought Betty Bell to herself, surveying the scene. 'And I'll take care not a morsel of that quince jam ever passes the innocent lips of poor dear Mr Shoosmith! My, that man just doesn't know what he's letting himself in for – coming to live at Thrush Green!'

Meanwhile, Miss Watson's assailant remained undetected.

The police had very little to go on. Miss Watson could tell them no more than she had at first, and there were no helpful footprints or finger-prints to help in the search. The weather had been brilliant and dry for over a month, and even if footprints had been left, the arrival of several dozen children at the school an hour or so later meant that a large number of them would be effaced. There seemed to be no doubt that the man had worn gloves, and indeed Miss Watson thought that she recalled that the cosh was gripped in an iron-grey woollen glove bound with leather.

She racked her aching brain for several days trying to pin down the faint sense of recognising those gloves and the man himself, but all was in vain. In the end she had given up worrying about it, and was content to take Miss Fogerty's good advice and 'let the matter rest.'

Miss Watson confessed that she could not have managed without Miss Fogerty's boundless help. Every morning the good little woman had arrived at eight o'clock to give her her breakfast in bed, until at the end of the week Miss Watson had insisted on returning to school again. There she had found everything in apple-pie order. The accounts had been kept, correspondence had been answered, fresh flowers decked the two classrooms and even the calendar had been torn off daily.

Miss Watson was much touched by her assistant's kindness and ability. Lying in bed for two or three days had given her, at last, time to dwell on the sterling qualities hidden beneath Miss Fogerty's mouse-like exterior. For twelve years she had taken the older woman for granted, and on many occasions had felt impatient with her timidity and out-of-date methods. At the end of each day she had bade farewell to Miss Fogerty with something akin to relief. Now it could never be quite the same again. Miss Fogerty had proved herself a friend.

As the headmistress limped about her school in the next few weeks she became increasingly aware of Miss Fogerty's newly-found confidence which had flowered during her own absence. The nervous acquiescence which had so often irritated Miss Watson had now vanished, and they discussed school problems on equal terms.

Misfortune had united and strengthened them both, and the school at Thrush Green was all the better for it.

The burglary had created some unease in the neighbourhood. People who had never locked a door in their lives now looked out forgotten keys and turned them in the locks before departing to Lulling for a morning's shopping. Those who had been in the habit of hiding their keys under upturned flower-pots or their door-scrapers now decided that it would be prudent to change these well-known hiding-places for new ones.

'I'm leaving my key under the mat in the back porch,' Mrs Bailey told her closest friends. 'Everyone knows about the ledge over the door.'

'We're putting ours behind the paraffin can in the shed now,' said Dimity.

Mr Piggott, who had a door key of ecclesiastical design weighing a good three-quarters of a pound, fixed it to a stout belt round his waist, and put up with the inconvenience of its sundry blows as he bent about his business in the churchyard. The burglary had impressed him considerably, and he made no bones about expressing his disgust with the police.

'What we pays them for I don't know,' he grumbled over his glass at 'The Two Pheasants.' 'Folks on Thrush Green going in fear of their lives – and what's done about it, eh? I'll lay I could find the chap that done it, if I was given half a chance!'

'That's right,' said the landlord, winking secretly at his other customers. 'You turn Sherlock Holmes, see – and show the police where they get off.'

As the last days of October slipped by, the press of autumn life caused the robbery to slip into the background. There were borders to be dug, wallflower plants to be put in, and all the outside preparations for winter which the kindly weather encouraged. Before long, Thrush Green would be enveloped in the cold rains and fogs of a Cotswold winter. If the weather prophets proved correct there would be snow too. Wise householders made the most of this respite, and the excitement of the newcomer to their midst and the attack on Miss Watson soon shook down into place with other matters.

But for old Mr Piggott the robbery was of major importance. He had lived alone ever since the departure of his daughter Molly with young Ben Curdle, and he had plenty of time to let his beer-befuddled imagination dwell on the mystery. As he pottered about his damp little cottage, or performed perfunctorily his simple duties as sexton of St Andrew's hard by, he dreamt wonderful day-dreams, envisaging himself as the sleuth of Thrush Green, the man who showed the police how to do their job, and the hero of his admiring and grateful neighbours.

'I'll show them,' muttered old Piggott, slashing viciously at a bed of nettles which threatened to engulf the headstone of Nathaniel Patten. 'I'll show them all – that I will!'

5. Nelly Tilling

THE day of the party dawned cold and blustery. Ella and Dimity sat at their breakfast table watching the bright leaves whirling to the grass. A spatter of rain rattled on the window-pane and Dimity shivered.

'Do you think we ought to light the paraffin stove in the sitting-room as well as the fire, dear?'

'Wouldn't be a bad idea to have it alight this morning, but we're not keeping that thing going all day. It'll smell the place out. Nothing like a strong reek for killing the party spirit.'

'But it doesn't smell!' protested Dimity.

'No woman thinks her own paraffin stove smells,' said Ella emphatically, dousing the stub of her cigarette in the dregs of her tea-cup. This detestable habit would have caused a less devoted companion to have left Ella long before, but Dimity daily shuddered and forbore to speak of her pain. 'It's a natural phenomenon,' continued Ella, blandly unaware of her friend's revulsion, 'like being unable to hear your own voice.'

Ella settled back comfortably, crossing one massive leg over the other, and seemed prepared to expand this interesting theory. But Dimity, conscious of the work to be done in preparation for the party, rose hastily and began to pack up the breakfast dishes.

'I think I'll get out Mother's little silver bon-bon dishes and polish them. They'll do beautifully for the salted nuts,' she began busily.

'They'll get tarnished,' objected Ella. 'What's wrong with saucers.'

'Saucers?' cried Dimity in horror. 'At a party?'

'I meant the *best* ones,' said Ella, trying vainly to bring down Dimity's heightened temperature.

'Quite out of the question!' replied Dimity, with unusual

severity. 'We must use the silver dishes, and I am quite prepared to polish them after the party.'

She might have added that no one in the household besides herself ever did do any polishing, but Dimity was used to holding her tongue and did not give way to temptation on this occasion.

Ella lumbered to her feet, sighing.

'Just as you say, Dim. You know best. Let's go and have a look at the decorations by daylight, and we'll see if we need the stove lighted.'

The two friends crossed the small hall to their sitting-room which they had embellished the previous evening. The fact that they had arranged the party for All Hallows E'en dawned on the two ladies soon after they had posted the invitations and Ella had put her ingenuity and skilled hands to work on the decorations.

A flight of witches, cut from stout black paper and dangling from threads, flew diagonally across the room, twisting and turning in the draughts in the most spirited manner. Their hair streamed behind them from their pointed hats, and Ella had stuck on green sequins for the eyes of her creations, which glittered balefully as they caught the light.

Two great copper jars filled with autumn leaves and Cape gooseberries glowed from the corners of the room, and on the mantelpiece stood a golden pumpkin. This had been presented by Dotty Harmer and Ella had hollowed it out, cut out two round eyes, a triangle for a nose and a crescent for a mouth, and put a night-light inside it. This, when lit, caused the hollow globe to glow and the whole effect was deliciously sinister.

Dimity looked at her friend's handiwork with genuine admiration.

'It's simply wonderful, Ella darling. I wonder if it would be a good idea to play a few Hallow E'en games – bobbing for apples, you know, and that kind of thing!' Dimity's faded eyes shone at the very thought, but her friend damped her ardour abruptly.

'Be your age, Dim! People are coming for a civilised glass of sherry and to meet their friends. They won't thank you for cold water down their bodices, ducking for green apples – and double pneumonia by the end of the week, ten chances to one.'

Her tone changed as she noted her friend's crestfallen face.

'We're all getting too long in the tooth for those capers,' she said more kindly. She patted Dimity's arm with a massive hand. 'Let's get the stove going for an hour or so, and check up on the drinks. Got any lemons, by the way?'

'Three,' said Dimity. 'Sevenpence each.' Her voice was still subdued and Ella wished she had been less brutal about poor old Dim's suggestion for games.

'It should be quite a cheerful crowd,' said Ella, trying to make amends. 'I'm glad the new man's coming.'

She led the way back to the dining-room with Dimity fluttering behind, and still looking like a kitten that has been kicked.

'Don't forget to look in the mirror when you brush your hair tonight, Dim,' continued Ella, with heavy jocularity. 'They say you see your husband on All Hallows E'en!'

The unconscious association of ideas in Ella's remarks might have struck an astute observer, but both Ella herself and Dimity were unaware of anything remarkable. To the two friends only one thing was apparent – the olive branch was being offered by one and gratefully accepted by the other.

With their arms affectionately entwined they approached the drinks cupboard.

The rain and wind increased as the morning wore on. The

honey-coloured houses that clustered round Thrush Green grew a deeper gold as the rain lashed their glistening walls. Thousands of drops ran from one Cotswold stone tile to the next, down the steep roofs to the waiting gutters which gurgled and spluttered with their unaccustomed load. Rain-water butts, which had stood almost empty for the past few weeks, rumbled and bubbled in their stout wooden bellies; and the thirsty gardens drank up the bounty and gave forth a blessed fragrance by way of grace.

Umbrellas bobbed down the hill to Lulling, and cars sent up flashing fountains from the long puddles by the side of the green. The horse-chestnut trees flailed their branches, sending down the last few leaves to join their fellows in the mud below.

The wind howled among the chimneys of Thrush Green, and the sign-board of 'The Two Pheasants' leant away to the south at a steep angle. Two tea towels in the little yard had twisted round and round the line until they looked like two bright giant caterpillars clinging there.

Above St Andrew's steeple a flock of rooks swayed and dipped in the airy tides. They looked like fragments of burnt paper eddying in the current from a bonfire, and now and again, above the roaring of the wind about them, a faint harsh cry could be heard.

Far below them, beneath the windy steeple, beneath the humming belfry with its singing louvres, and beneath the draughty chancel, Mr Piggott, like some earthy mole, laboured in the stoke-hole.

Here was no sound of wind and storm, no icy splash of rain. The great boiler gave forth a pungent heat and whispered quietly as it digested its coke.

Nearby stood its guardian. Mr Piggott had two clothes pegs in his mouth and his spare shirt in his hands. A row of garments sagged from a small line and steamed gently in the heat.

Mr Piggott's wash-day took no account of the weather. The heat which he engendered to warm the worshippers might just as well dry his clothes, argued the sexton to himself, as he pegged the shirt on the line.

Standing back, he surveyed his clothes with pride. They might not be as white as those of his neighbours which he saw billowing on their lines, but here, among the coke, they looked all right to Mr Piggott.

He took out a large watch and squinted at it short-sightedly. Surely they must be open by now! He saw, with pleasure, that the hands stood at ten-thirty.

With remarkable agility Mr Piggott mounted the steep stone stairs from the stoke-hole, and prepared to face the weather.

The noise above ground surprised him. There was a menacing hum high in the lofty dimness above him, and a general confused roaring from the trees outside the church. Mr Piggott made his way up the long aisle, bending here and there to pick up a stray dead leaf or morsel of confetti which the wind had flung in from outside. While he was thus engaged he became conscious of other noises nearer at hand. He heard the metallic click of the porch door, the clanking which betokened heavy feet on the wire foot-scraper and the gasping of a breathless wayfarer.

'Treading in the dirt all over my flagstones,' muttered Mr Piggott, inhospitably, opening the heavy church door with a venomous tug. There was a squeal of surprise as the newcomer turned to face him, her hand on her capacious bosom.

'Lor, Albert, you give me a fright!' puffed the lady. 'Never 'ad no idea of you being in there. Came in out of the wet for half a minute. All right, is it?'

She darted a quick look at the sexton from small dark eyes well embedded in rosy flesh. Beneath her sodden head-scarf a few dark curls protruded, sparkling with rain-drops. She seated herself on the stone bench and began to peel off her wet gloves.

Mr Piggott watched sourly. He had known Nelly Tilling most of his life, and they had shared the same desk at the village school for a term or two. Kept her looks, she had, observed Mr Piggott privately, if you liked them plump. Why, she must weigh nigh on twelve or thirteen stone, he ruminated, casting an eye experienced in assessing the weight of a pig, over his old school-fellow's bulk.

'Don't want to sit on that stone,' advised Mr Piggott, dourly. 'Strikes up.'

'Well, it does a bit,' confessed the lady, heaving herself to her feet. 'But I'm real whacked, walking against this wind.'

'Best come inside, I suppose,' said Mr Piggott, grudgingly, but he made no move to open the door. He found his visitor a nuisance. Should he invite her down to the stoke-hole to dry out, he wondered? Thoughts of his dangling underclothes dismayed him. He had no desire to be the butt of Nelly Tilling's derision. His own cottage was cold and he did not want his neighbours to see him taking the buxom widow into it, for Nelly Tilling was reputed to be looking for a second husband after burying her first the year before, and Mr Piggott disliked appearing ridiculous. If he invited her to 'The Two Pheasants' he would have to pay for her, and that, of course, was unthinkable.

On the other hand, Mr Piggott was surprised to feel a tiny glow within him as he watched Mrs Tilling shaking her gloves and brushing the drops from her enormous coat. After all, they had been to school together, it was a beast of a day, and the poor toad was likely to catch her death if she sat about in those clammy things without a sup in her. And, say what you liked, she was a fine-looking woman and Mr Piggott realised, with a shock, that he had felt lonely for a long time. Somewhat to his horror, he heard himself saying:

'Come and join me in a drink. I was on my way to "The Two Pheasants." '

The lady's reaction to this innocent suggestion was alarming. Her rosy face became redder than ever, her dark eyes flashed fire, and indignation swelled her heaving breast to such an extent that her coat buttons strained from the cloth. She reminded Mr Piggott of a bridling turkey-cock.

'I joined the Band of Hope the same day as you did, if you can cast your mind back that far, Albert Piggott! And what's more, I ain't never broke the pledge yet – which is more than you can say from what I hear!'

She advanced upon the shrinking sexton to wag a massive finger in his face. Mr Piggott backed away nervously until his greasy cap knocked against a bland cherub who stared sightlessly from the porch wall. Nelly Tilling, in anger, was an awe-inspiring sight. She seemed akin to the natural elements which raged so furiously around her, and though taken aback at her onslaught, Mr Piggott found himself admiring her spirit.

'No need to act so spiteful then,' returned the sexton, with unusual mildness. He rubbed his knocked head while he reviewed the situation.

Nelly Tilling calmed down a little after her outburst and withdrew to study the weather from the doorway. Behind her sturdy shoulders Mr Piggott caught a glimpse of the inn's sign-board as it groaned and creaked in the gale. His thirst returned.

'Well, gal, if you don't want a drop, I do,' he said ungallantly. 'Make yourself at home here, while I slip over. Stoking's thirsty work, and I ain't never made no boast about taking the pledge!'

He made to edge past her, but the lady turned to face him, barring his way. Her red mouth was curved in a delicious smile. Albert Piggott found it both alarming and bewitching.

' 'Ere, let me—' he began weakly.

'Albert, I wouldn't say no to a nice cup of tea, if I was to be asked over to your house. How about it?'

Mr Piggott's fear of his neighbours' interest must have made itself apparent in his apprehensive face.

' 'Twould only be civil, a day like this,' pressed Nelly Tilling. 'I wouldn't stop more than a minute or two – just while the rain's so heavy.'

Mr Piggott's expression lightened a trifle, but his mouth still turned down at the corners.

'I can't stop long in any case,' pursued Nelly, winningly. 'I've left a sheep's head boiling on the stove.'

Mr Piggott allowed a half-smile to soften his severity.

'Sheep's head!' he whispered huskily. 'Why, I haven't had a bite of sheep's head since my Molly got wed!' His rheumy old eyes gazed unseeingly into the windy distance behind Nelly's head.

Mrs Tilling gave a violent shiver and a very creditable imitation of a sneeze.

'I'm in for a cold if I don't get a hot drink soon,' said she, pathetically. Her dark eyes gazed at her old school-fellow with all the wistful appeal of a beaten spaniel's.

Mr Piggott succumbed.

'Come on over then,' he said bravely, opening the porch door. A vicious burst of wind almost buffeted the breath from them and the rain danced like spinning silver coins on the old flagged path.

'Put your head down, Nell, and we'll run for it,' shouted the sexton.

* * *

Wind-blown and panting, Mrs Tilling thankfully accepted the armchair which Mr Piggott indicated.

'I'll just tidy these up,' said her host, stuffing a dozen or so unwashed socks behind the grubby cushion. Mrs Tilling viewed the proceedings with some misgivings, but sat herself down gingerly on the edge of the seat.

'Make yerself at 'ome,' said Mr Piggott, passing her an out-of-date copy of the parish magazine. 'I'll put on the kettle.'

He moved into the little kitchen which led from the sitting-room and soon Nelly could hear the tap running. Her eyes wandered round the unsavoury room. If ever a house cried out for a woman's hand, thought the lady dramatically, this was it!

She noted the greasy chenille tablecloth which was thread-bare where the table edge cut into it – a sure sign, Nelly knew, that the cloth had been undisturbed for many months. Her eyes travelled to the dead fern in its arid pot, the ashes in the rusty grate, the festoons of cobwebs which hung from filthy pelmets to picture rails and the appalling thickness of the dust which covered the drab objects on the dresser.

The only cheerful spot of colour in the room was afforded by St Andrew's church almanack which Mr Piggott had fixed on the wall above the rickety card table which supported an ancient wireless set.

Mrs Tilling, who began to find the room oppressive and smelly, left her sock-laden armchair (from whence, she suspected, most of the aroma emanated), and decided to investigate the kitchen.

Mr Piggott was standing morosely by the kettle waiting for it to boil. It was typical of a man, thought his guest with some impatience, that he had not utilised his time by putting out the cups and saucers, milk, sugar and so on, which would be needed. Just like poor old George, thought Nelly with a pang, remembering her late husband. 'One thing at a time,' he used to say pompously, as though there were some virtue in it. As his wife had pointed out tartly, on many occasions, she herself would never get through a quarter of her quota of work if she indulged herself in such idleness. While a kettle boiled she could set a table, light a fire, and watch over a cooking breakfast. Ah, men were poor tools, thought Mrs Tilling!

The kitchen was even dirtier than its neighbour. A sour fustiness pervaded the dingy room. In a corner on the floor stood a saucer of milk which had long since turned to an unsavoury junket embellished with blue mould. Beside it lay two very dead herrings' heads. A mound of dirty crockery hid the draining-board, and the sight of Mr Piggott's frying pan hanging on the wall was enough to turn over Mrs Tilling's stout stomach. The residue of dozens of past meals could here be seen embedded in grey fat. Slivers of black burnt onion, petrified bacon rinds, lacy brown scraps of fried eggs and scores of other morsels from tomatoes, sausages, steaks, chops, liver, potatoes, bread and beans here lay cheek by jowl and would have afforded a rich reward to anyone interested in Mr Piggott's diet over the past year.

'Where d'you keep the cups?' asked Nelly Tilling, when she had regained her breath. Her gaze turned apprehensively towards the pile on the draining-board. Mr Piggott seemed to sense her misgivings.

'Got some in the other room, in the dresser cupboard,' he said. 'My old woman's best,' he explained. 'Molly used 'em sometimes.'

'You get them while I make the tea,' said Mrs Tilling briskly. 'This the pot?' She peered into the murky depths of a battered tin object on the stove.

'Ah! Tea's in,' said Mr Piggott, making his way to the dresser.

The kettle boiled. With a brave shudder Nelly poured the

water on the tea leaves, comforting herself with the thought that boiling water killed germs of all sorts.

Five minutes later she put down her empty cup and smiled at her companion.

'Lovely cup of tea,' she said truthfully. 'I feel all the better for that. Now I must go over to Doctor Lovell's for my pills.'

'It's still pouring,' said Mr Piggott. 'Have another cup.'

'I'll pour,' said Nelly. 'Pass your own.'

'It's nice to have someone to pour out,' confessed Mr Piggott. He was beginning to feel unaccountably cheerful despite the disappointment of missing his customary pint of beer. 'This place needs a woman.'

'I'll say it does!' agreed Nelly, warmly. 'It needs a few gallons of hot soapy water too! When did your Molly see this last?'

'About a year ago, I suppose. She's coming again Christmas-time – she and Ben and the baby. Maybe she'll give it a bit of a clean-up then.'

'It wouldn't hurt you to do a bit,' said Nelly roundly. 'Chuck out that milk and fish, for one thing.'

'The cat ain't had nothing to eat for days,' objected her host, stung by her criticism.

'That don't surprise me,' retorted Nelly. 'No cat would stay in this hole.'

'I got me church to see to,' began Mr Piggott, truculently. 'I ain't got time to—'

'If Molly comes home to this mess at Christmas then I'm sorry for her,' asserted Mrs Tilling. 'And the baby too. Like as not it'll catch something and die on your very hearth-stone!'

She paused to let the words sink in. Mr Piggott mumbled gloomily to himself. The gist of his mutterings was the unpleasantness of women, their officiousness, their fussiness and their inability to let well alone, but he took care to keep his remarks inaudible.

'Tell you what,' said Mrs Tilling in a warmer tone. 'I'll come up here and give you a hand turning out before Christmas. What about it?'

Mr Piggott's forebodings returned. What would the neighbours say? What was Nelly Tilling up to? What would happen to his own peaceful, slummocky bachelor existence if he allowed this woman to have her way?

Nelly watched the thoughts chasing each other across his dour countenance. After a few minutes she noticed a certain cunning softness replacing the apprehension of his expression, and her heart began to beat a little faster.

'No harm, I suppose,' said the old curmudgeon, grudgingly. 'Make things a bit more welcoming for Molly, wouldn't it?'

'That's right,' agreed Mrs Tilling, rising from her chair and brushing a fine collection of sticky crumbs from her coat. 'One good turn deserves another, you know, and we've been friends long enough to act neighbourly, haven't we, Albert?'

Mr Piggott found himself quite dazzled by the warmth of her smile as she made for the door, and was unable to speak.

The wind roared in as she opened the front door, lifting the filthy curtains and blowing the parish magazine into a corner. Might freshen the place up a bit, thought Nelly, stepping out into the storm.

'Thanks for the tea, Albert. I'll drop in again when I'm passing,' shouted the lady, as she retreated into the uproar.

Mr Piggott nodded dumbly, shut the door with a crash, and breathed deeply. Mingled pleasure and fury shook his aged frame, but overriding all these agitations was the urgent need for a drink.

'Women!' spat out Mr Piggott, resuming his damp raincoat. 'Never let a chap alone!'

His mind turned the phrase over. There was something about it that made Mr Piggott feel younger – a beau, a masher, a man who was still pursued.

'Never let a chap alone!' repeated Mr Piggott aloud. He pulled on his wet cap, adjusting it at an unusually rakish and dashing angle, and made his way, swaggering very slightly, to his comforts next door.

'Do you know,' said Dimity Dean, looking up from polishing the silver baskets ready for the evening's festivities, 'do you know that Nelly Tilling has just come out of Piggott's house?'

'Nelly Tilling?' repeated Ella, looking up from rolling an untidy cigarette. 'Which is she?'

'You know,' said Dimity, with some impatience. 'The fat woman who's supposed to be looking for a second husband!'

'Hm!' grunted Ella shortly. 'She's welcome to old Piggott!'

6. All Hallows E'en

AT six-thirty Ella and Dimity awaited their guests. Both ladies were dressed in the frocks which had been recognised by Thrush Green and Lulling as their cocktail clothes for the last decade, and both exuded the aroma of their recent baths, lavender in Dimity's case and Wright's Coal Tar soap in Ella's.

Dimity's grey crêpe had a cowl neck-line which had been rather fashionable just after the war and a full skirt which a more sophisticated woman would have supported with a stiffened petticoat. Over Dimity's modest Vedonis straight petticoat, however, the fullness draped itself limply, ending in a hem so uneven that it was obviously the work of the cleaner's rather than the couturier's. A rose of squashed fawn silk at the waist-line strove unavailingly to add dash to this ensemble.

Ella, in a plain black woollen frock decorated only with cigarette ash on the bodice, looked surprisingly elegant. Released for once from their brogues her feet were remarkably neat in a pair of black suède shoes, low-heeled but well-cut, which drew attention to the fact that despite Ella's bulk she still showed an attractive pair of ankles.

The fire crackled and blazed hospitably giving forth a sweet smell of burning apple wood. The golden pumpkin glowed on the mantelpiece, its grotesque face beaming a welcome. Ella counted the bottles briskly and busied herself with bottle opener, lemons and glasses, while Dimity fluttered hither and thither putting little dishes of salted nuts and other savoury things first here, then there, surveying the effect with much anguish.

'All I want,' said Ella, squinting at her companion over the cigarette smoke which curled into her eye, 'is a private dish of olives behind the azalea. I've seen that young Lovell at parties before, wolfing 'em down. By the time I've got the drinks circulating he'll have had the lot,' said his hostess forthrightly.

'Oh, Ella dear,' protested Dimity, 'I'm quite sure he doesn't behave like that! He's a very well-brought-up young man.' But she obediently put one dish of olives behind the azalea plant near Ella, nevertheless. Ella took three, clapped them into her mouth, like a man taking pills, and crunched with relish.

'I'll bet you sixpence in the Cats' Protection box that Dotty arrives first,' said Ella rather indistinctly.

'Of course she'll be first,' said Dimity. 'It's not worth betting on. Besides,' she added, looking thoughtful, 'I don't know that we ought to bet like that. The rector was saying, only the other day, that betting is on the increase.'

'Bless his innocent old heart,' cried Ella, wiping her olive-wet palm smartly down the side of her skirt, 'what on earth is he doing then when he holds a raffle for the organ fund?'

'It's not quite the same—' began Dimity primly, when the bell rang and both ladies hurried to meet their first guest. It was, as they had surmised, their old friend Dotty Harmer, clad in her familiar seal-skin jacket. This archaic garment had been her mother's, and had an old-world charm with its nipped-in waist and a hint of leg-of-mutton about the upper part of the sleeves.

'Come in, come in,' shouted Ella hospitably, throwing open the door with such violence that the house shook.

'I'll just take off my boots on the step,' said Dotty, bending over. 'It's absolutely filthy along my field path after all the rain. What a day – what a day!'

'You come in,' said Ella, in a slightly hectoring manner. 'It's perishing in this wind, stripped out as we are. Besides, we'll have the fire smoking.'

Thus adjured, Dotty pressed into the little hall and the front door was shut against the roaring night.

'They're my *new* boots,' explained Dotty proudly. 'I put them on *over* my shoes, you see, and then I can just step out easily and I don't dirty people's carpets.' Her wrinkled old face was flushed with excitement. She might have been six years old in her unaffected delight.

'How awfully sensible,' said Dimity kindly, watching her friend tugging ineffectually at one boot while she balanced precariously on the other. 'Can I help?'

'I'll just sit on the stairs,' said Dotty. 'They're a bit stiff.'

'Come inside,' implored Ella, rubbing her hands for warmth. It was apparent to her that Dotty would be stuck on the stairs in everybody's way, puffing and blowing over her infernal boots, for some time to come. 'Or upstairs to the bedroom.'

'But that *entirely* defeats the purpose of my boots,' protested Dotty. 'I shan't be a moment.'

She bent down again, her face becoming purple with her efforts.

'Let me—' began Dimity, but Dotty waved her aside.

'No, no, no! It's just their being new,' puffed Dotty, resting one thin leg across the other knee and displaying an alarming amount of undergarments to the glass front door. Really, thought Ella irritably, she carries eccentricity too far. In two shakes we shall have the others arriving – the new man among them – and it's enough to frighten a stranger out of his wits to see old Dotty mopping and mowing in her seal-skin coat with one boot in her ear. Her irritation, coupled with the draughts in the tiny hall, gave Ella inspiration.

'Take the whole thing off, Dotty, shoe and all. Then you can pull your shoe out afterwards.'

The other two ladies gazed at her with respect. Dotty obeyed, the shoes were retrieved, her jacket taken from her, and Dotty stood revealed in the brick-coloured dress and coral necklace whose fine divergence of shade had delighted the neighbourhood for so long.

'Oh, my jacket!' wailed Dotty, as she was being ushered into the sitting-room. 'I've brought you some of my quince jam, dears. It's in the pocket.'

'How kind,' said Dimity. 'I'll put it in the kitchen at once.' She fluttered off on her errand, leaving Dotty to exclaim over the metamorphosis of her pumpkin.

Guests now began to arrive thick and fast and the little sitting-room was soon filled with chatter and laughter. All those present had known each other for years and more than half of them had met before during the day as they went about their daily rounds. Harold Shoosmith had not yet arrived and Ella wondered if he could have forgotten, as she bore her tray of drinks round the room.

The small clock on the mantelpiece was striking seven when

the door-bell shrilled and Ella and Dimity hurried to answer it.

Harold Shoosmith entered in a gust of wind and a shower of apologies. The telephone had rung as he was about to leave – a long-distance call – an old friend in trouble – on her way north and had shattered her windscreen – might call at his house later. The words gushed out as Ella took his coat and scarf so that it was some minutes before she could introduce him to Dimity who stood looking pink and expectant at the sight of such a handsome – and unattached – man actually under her own roof.

Harold Shoosmith gave Dimity a smile that turned her heart over, murmured some polite words and followed his hostesses into the sitting-room, smoothing his white hair, which the wind had ruffled, as he went. His dark suit was impeccably cut, his linen snowy, his tie discreetly striped, and denoted, both ladies felt sure, a school, college or regiment of the finest quality. They felt very proud of their distinguished guest as they led him to their friends and Dimity felt, for the first time, that it was a pity that Thrush Green men did not take the same pains with their dressing. Why, young Doctor Lovell, she noticed now, was actually wearing a dog-tooth checked jacket with leather patches on the sleeves! But, of course, she chided herself hastily, he may have come straight from a patient's sick bed. One must be charitable.

The newcomer was soon happily settled with a gin and tonic and Doctor Bailey and the rector to talk to. Very soon Doctor Lovell and his brother-in-law Edward Young, who was a local architect, drifted towards the group and Ella saw, with some resignation, that the sexes had divided into two camps as usual.

She made her way to the ladies' end to replenish Violet Lovelock's glass. The three Miss Lovelocks had seated themselves on the window-seat, their silvery heads nodding and trembling, and their glasses, as Ella expected, quite empty.

These three ladies, now in their seventies, lived in a Georgian doll's house in Lulling's High Street. There they had been born, their wicker bassinette had been bumped down the shallow flight of steps to the pavement by their trim nursemaid, young men had called, but not one of the three tall sisters had emerged from the house as a bride. They lived together peaceably enough, busying themselves with good works and their neighbours' affairs, and collecting *objets d'art* for their over-crowded gem of a house with a ruthless zeal which was a by-word for miles around.

Many a hostess had found herself bereft of a lustre jug or a particularly charming paper-weight when the Misses Lovelock rose to leave, for they had brought the art of persuasive begging to perfection. Continuously crying poverty, they lived nevertheless very comfortably, and the inhabitants of Lulling and Thrush Green were wary of these genteel old harpies. Tales were exchanged of the Lovelocks' exploits.

One told of their kind offer to look after her garden while she was away and how she came back to find it stripped of all the ripe fruit and the choicest vegetables. 'Such a pity, dear, to see it going to waste. We knew you would like us to help ourselves, and it does keep the crop growing, of course. We must let you have a bottle of the raspberries – so delicious.'

Neighbours who were unwary enough to let the Misses Lovelock look after the chickens in their absence rarely found any eggs awaiting them on their return, and in some cases a plump chicken had died. 'Terribly upsetting, my dear! It was just lying on its poor back with its legs stuck up and a dreadfully resigned look on its dear face! We buried it in our garden as we didn't want to upset you.'

The ladies now smiled gently upon Ella as she retrieved their glasses. All three were drinking whisky, barely moistened with soda water, with a rapidity that had ceased to startle their friends. Ella noticed, with some alarm, that their eyes were fixed upon the silver basket which Dimity was proffering.

'Do you like salted nuts, Bertha?' asked Dimity anxiously of the youngest Miss Lovelock. Bertha, Ada and Violet took two or three daintily in their claw-like hands. Their eyes remained appraisingly upon the gleaming little dish.

'What a charming little basket!' murmured Violet.

'We have its brother at home,' said Ada, very sweetly. 'I believe this should be one of a pair.'

'I can see we shall have to ask Dimity to take pity on our poor lonely little dish at home!' tinkled Bertha, laughing gently.

Ella broke in with bluff good humour.

'Better bring your lonely one up here! We've got a couple to keep it company, haven't we, Dim?'

The three sisters tittered politely and took refreshing gulps of whisky, while Dimity cast a grateful look at her protector and made her escape to young Mrs Lovell, clutching her mother's silver basket to the fawn silk rose.

Ruth Lovell was a great favourite of hers. Dimity had known her since she was a little girl and had shared Thrush Green's delight at her marriage with Doctor Lovell a year ago.

Ruth looked young and glowing with health. Dimity remembered her wan sad demeanour some years before when the poor girl had been cruelly jilted and she had come to recuperate with her sister Joan Young, and, soon after, had found consolation with Doctor Bailey's new junior partner.

'What a long time since we've met, Ruth,' said Dimity, sitting down beside the girl. 'And how pretty you look in that pink blouse! I like the way you young things wear your blouses loose over your skirts or trousers. It's really most becoming. And I really believe you are putting on a little weight, my dear, which suits you so well.' She patted Ruth's knee encouragingly.

'It's only to be expected, Dimity,' replied Ruth, smiling. 'You know we're looking forward to a baby at Christmas-time. That's why I'm in this enormous smock. Nothing else fits!'

Dimity's eyes grew round and she grew pink with pleasure and embarrassment.

'How perfectly lovely, my dear! Do you know, I hadn't heard a word of it. Now isn't that extraordinary? But I do so hope the men didn't hear me making such thoughtless remarks to you.' She looked anxiously towards the other end of the room where the men stood in a cloud of blue tobacco smoke making an immense amount of noise.

'Don't worry,' said Ruth. 'They're far too engrossed. Now, you must promise to be one of the very first to see the baby. I shall look forward to seeing you particularly.'

Dimity nodded delightedly and, looking conspiratorial, went to see how the men were faring.

* * *

'It was one of the reasons why I chose Thrush Green to live in,' Harold Shoosmith was saying. 'I've the greatest admiration for Nathaniel Patten, and to find a house for sale in his birthplace seemed too good a chance to miss.'

'A wonderful person,' agreed the rector. The round blue eyes in his chubby face gazed up at his new parishioner's great height. The rector of Thrush Green bore a striking resemblance to the cherubs which decorated his church and his disposition was as child-like and innocent as theirs. He was a man blessed with true humility and warm with charity. From the top of his shining bald head to the tips of his small black shoes he radiated a happiness that disarmed all comers. Thrush Green was rightly proud of the Reverend Charles Henstock, and watched his tubby little figure traversing his parish, with much affection.

'You know, of course,' said Harold Shoosmith, to the group at large, 'that it's the hundredth anniversary of Nathaniel's birth next March.'

'I didn't know,' said Edward Young honestly.

'Nor me,' said Doctor Lovell. 'Tell me, who was the old boy?'

'Now that's quite shocking,' chided old Doctor Bailey laughingly. 'Nathaniel Patten is a public figure. He was a most zealous missionary. Am I right?' he appealed to Harold Shoosmith.

'Indeed you are,' said he. 'He founded a wonderful mission station in the town where I worked overseas. They were making great plans for all kinds of festivities in March. They hope to add a wing to their hospital on the occasion.'

'We really should do something ourselves,' said the rector, wrinkling his brow. 'I must confess I hadn't given it the thought I should, though I certainly intended to put a brief note in the parish magazine for that month.'

'He was an amazingly fine person,' said Harold Shoosmith.

'It seems a pity if his anniversary goes by unnoticed in his birthplace. It won't elsewhere, I can assure you.'

'We might consider putting up a small plaque,' suggested Edward Young. 'In the church perhaps, or on his house.' He looked suddenly thoughtful. 'If anyone knows which house he was born in,' he added doubtfully.

'I think you'll find it is one of the cottages by "The Two Pheasants," ' said Harold Shoosmith. 'Doesn't the sexton live in one there somewhere?'

'Indeed he does,' agreed the rector. 'I must find out more about Nathaniel Patten. It is shameful to know so little about Thrush Green's most distinguished son.'

'I've collected a few notes about him,' said the newcomer. 'Call in any time and I'll let you have them. I do feel that it would be an excellent thing to remind Thrush Green of Nathaniel's place in the world. I should be very glad to do anything to help in the way of celebrating his anniversary.'

The rector thanked him and promised to call. Edward Young wondered if Piggott's cottage would stand up to a ladder against it, if a plaque were to be affixed on its ancient face. Doctor Lovell made a mental note to ask his wife if she had ever heard of this old missionary fellow who had made so deep an impression on Harold Shoosmith. Doctor Bailey turned his mind back to his early days at Thrush Green, and tried to remember, unavailingly, if Nathaniel Patten's daughter had once been among his patients, and if so, what her married name was. He must ask Winnie, he told himself, when they were home again.

Meanwhile, Dimity, who had hovered on the edge of the group listening to the conversation, now found a chance to collect the men's glasses.

'This is a delightful room,' said Harold Shoosmith, as he took the tray from her grasp and carried it towards Ella. 'And this is the happiest evening I've had since coming to Thrush Green.'

Suddenly, for Dimity, the fire crackled more gaily, the pumpkin beamed more brightly, and the glasses tinkled and sparkled with twice as much gaiety. It was a perfect party, she told herself, with an upsurging of spirits. Let the wind scream outside, let the rain lash the window panes! Here within, was warmth and colour, the comfort of old friends, and the excitement of new ones.

7. The Newcomer Settles In

HAROLD SHOOSMITH soon found, as all newcomers to a village find, that there was plenty to do. During his busy working days abroad, he had occasionally dwelt upon the peaceful bliss of his retirement in England. He imagined himself pottering about an English garden, discussing with an enthusiastic hard-working gardener the planting of new rose beds or an embryo orchard, or the best way to train an espalier pear on the south wall. He dallied with the idea of collecting china – possibly the attractive little houses used for burning pastilles, for which he had always felt a great affection – and had seen himself, in fancy, picking his entranced way among the well-dusted shelves in the drawing-room which housed his purchases.

He looked forward to entertaining in a modest way, a simple supper for his friends, or perhaps a tea-party for those with children. He realised that domestic help might be difficult to find, but in all these rosy dreams there lurked somewhere in the background a competent but self-effacing servant.

His decision to settle in Thrush Green was prompted, as he

told the vicar, by his admiration for Nathaniel Patten and the fortuitous advertisement about the corner house which was published at a time when he was beginning to feel anxious about finding a suitable resting place. The matter was arranged quickly, and his dreams seemed to be very near at last.

Reality came as a shock. The garden, which was in an appalling state of neglect by the time he arrived, looked like staying that way for all the help Harold Shoosmith was likely to find. He was not averse to digging, weeding, hoeing and pruning, but he knew that the job was much too large for him to tackle alone, and also he needed the advice of some local person about soil, drainage, and reliable sources of plants, shrubs and garden needs such as manure, leaf-mould and so on. An advertisement in the local paper brought two replies. One was from a middle-aged lady in riding breeches, with metallic yellow hair sporting a wide dark parting, whose appearance so startled Mr Shoosmith that he felt quite unequal to considering her application. He told her suavely, and untruthfully, that the place was already taken, and had many uncomfortable meetings with her later at various cocktail parties. The second applicant was so old, so shaky, and had so rheumy and red an eye that he had difficulty in supporting himself in Mr Shoosmith's presence, let alone a gardening tool, even of the lightest construction.

Diligent enquiries among his neighbours at Thrush Green and Lulling brought forth nothing, and in the end Harold Shoosmith realised that he must consider himself lucky if that old rogue Piggott deigned to call in for an hour or two to make a little extra beer money.

As for help in the house, that too, he found, was practically non-existent. The deft and devoted cook and housemaid whom he had been prepared to engage – provided that their references were first-class, of course – were replaced by Betty Bell, and he knew that he was fortunate to have her somewhat slap-dash ministrations. He was a sensible man, who soon realised that he had been living in a fool's paradise, and he accepted his present mode of living very cheerfully, becoming very fond of chatty Betty Bell and quite resigned to the fact that any collection he might make would be comfortably covered with dust unless he set to and dusted it himself.

Picking up pastille houses on his travels for a shilling or two, was yet another dream that was abruptly shattered. The price of any worthwhile small piece was beyond Harold Shoosmith's straitened means, he discovered. As for entertaining, his plans for simple supper parties of two or three well-cooked courses soon evaporated, and he was content to offer a drink and a cigarette to his neighbours, in the usual Thrush Green manner.

His time was much taken up with small domestic chores for which he found he had some natural aptitude. He chopped firewood, carried coal, swept the paths, painted the gates and fences, and found himself extremely busy. By the time evening came he was often quite tired and prepared to go up to bed by ten o'clock. If life in England did not have the leisurely nineteenth-century flavour which he had so fondly imagined might still exist in its rural backwaters, yet it was very pleasant, nevertheless, and Harold Shoosmith faced his years of retirement contentedly enough.

The number of local activities brought to Harold Shoosmith's notice, in the first few weeks of his residence at the corner house, as in need of his support, staggered him. In Thrush Green and Lulling were to be found Guides, Scouts, Brownies, Cubs, a Church Guild, a Chapel Youth Centre, a Mothers' Union, a Women's Institute, and no end of functions instigated by various sporting clubs.

He found himself giving clothing to three minute Brownies

with a hand-cart for their jumble sale, lending his ladder to the Scouts for the repair of their Den roof and giving half-crowns to various worthy people who called with a collecting tin. On one occasion he even agreed, under pressure, to parting with a newly-baked chocolate sponge which Betty Bell informed him he had promised as his contribution to the Sunday School party.

This was not all. He was urged by the rector, Doctor Lovell, and many other residents to join the committees of at least a dozen local bodies. Their pleas were so ardent that Harold Shoosmith wondered how on earth they had managed to get along at all without his help for so many years. The most pressing need, it seemed, was that of Thrush Green's Entertainment Committee which, the rector said solemnly, 'was in need of new blood.'

He had called upon Mr Shoosmith one wet November evening, splashing through the puddles of the newly-gravelled drive in the early darkness.

The bright blaze of October had changed to a succession of dreary days in November, each bringing hours of heavy rain which soon turned the green into a quagmire and sent rivers gurgling continuously along the gutters. Wellingtons and mackintoshes were the daily wear, the men working in the fields were soaked daily, and at the village school a row of wet gloves steamed on the fireguard every morning. Gardeners stood at their windows fuming at their neglected gardens. The heavy clay soil of the Cotswolds became impossible to turn in its glutinous condition. The last of the flowers lay battered on the sodden ground and the cows in the fields stood patiently, backs to the wind and rain, with water trickling steadily from their glistening coats. The water ran so continuously from the thatched roofs of one or two of Thrush Green's cottages that the stones beneath were scoured as clean as if they were in the bed of a trout stream. Tempers grew frayed as wet day followed wet day and washing had to be dried by the fire. The women were at their wits' end to keep up with the demand for dry clothing, and the windows were opaque with steam both by day and night.

'Appalling weather,' said Harold Shoosmith, settling his friend by the fire. His eye was caught by the rector's sodden shoes which squelched as he moved. The soles, he observed, were in sore need of mending. The fellow wants looking after, thought Harold Shoosmith.

'Would you like to borrow some slippers? We could dry your shoes while you're here.'

The rector's cherubic face became pinker and he looked concerned.

'I do so hope I haven't made a mess on your carpets. I quite forgot how dirty it was outside.'

His companion reassured him on this point but was unable to persuade him to part with his disgraceful foot-gear which steamed gently in the glow from the fire. The rector settled back in his leather armchair and looked with pleasure about the room.

'You've made it all uncommonly cosy,' he remarked. Betty Bell's ministrations were apparent in the gleaming copper kettle on the hearth and the array of silver cups which reflected the firelight on the sideboard opposite the hearth. Harold Shoosmith had been something of an athlete in his younger days, and this was another bond that the two men had, for Mr Henstock had once coxed his college eight in the years when he had weighed seven and a half stone.

He found Harold Shoosmith's comfortable house and his friendly welcome particularly cheering. The Reverend Charles Henstock, although he did not realise it, was much lonelier than he imagined. The death of his wife, some years before, had been borne with great courage. His religion was of the greatest comfort to him, for he was sustained by the knowledge that he would meet his wife again as soon as he left this world for the next. The affection and kindness of his parishioners never ceased to amaze him. The thought that his own shining honesty, modesty and goodwill might be the cause of his neighbours' esteem never entered his head. He was welcomed in all the houses in his parish, but felt some hesitation in staying too long. Fathers were coming home from work, children from school, wives from shopping. He, who had no wife and no child in his home, found the company of the newcomer to Thrush Green much to his liking. They were roughly the same age, enjoyed the same pleasures and had plenty of time on their own. It was natural that the rector began to call more and more frequently at the corner house. For his part, Harold Shoosmith liked his pastor more each time they met.

'I've been thinking about the memorial to Nathaniel Patten,' said the rector, warming his hands at the fire. 'The subject came up at the last meeting of the Entertainments Committee.'

'How did that come about?' asked Harold, much amused.

'We were discussing the arrangements for the Fur and Feather—' began the rector earnestly.

'The Fur and Feather?' ejaculated his friend, looking up from poking the fire. 'What on earth's that? A pub?'

'No, no! "The Fur and Feather *Whist Drive*," I should have said,' the rector explained. 'We have one every Christmas in the village school.'

'But why "Fur and Feather"?' persisted the wanderer in other lands. 'What's the significance of calling it that?'

The rector began to explain patiently that the prizes for this particular type of whist drive were of poultry or game. His friend's brow cleared.

'I see. Thank you. But how does this tie up with Nathaniel?'

'Well, you know what village meetings are – everything is discussed except the points on the agenda. I find it very helpful in my parish work. I always get to hear who is ill or in trouble of any sort. It's most necessary for a parish priest to be on committees. I really don't know how I'd manage without them.'

'Is the idea acceptable, then?'

'Indeed it is. General feeling seems to be in favour of a really worthwhile memorial. I suggested a seat on the green, but most people seem to think that a statue is the thing.'

'Pretty expensive, I imagine. And it might turn out to be hideous.'

'We might get someone in the neighbourhood to do it,' said the rector vaguely. 'Miss Bembridge is very artistic.'

'Good God!' said Harold, startled into strong language. 'D'you mean she'd do it?'

'She hasn't been approached, of course,' replied Mr Henstock. 'But I believe it has been suggested.'

A heavy silence fell upon the room. The rector was trying to remember just what it was that he meant to ask his new friend to do for him. Harold Shoosmith, glumly surveying the crack which he had just widened so successfully in a large lump of coal, was blind to the delights of the hissing gaseous flames which fluttered like yellow crocuses in the crevices. A memorial to his beloved Nathaniel Patten was one thing – a ghastly monstrosity created by the intimidating Ella was another. He shuddered to think where his first innocent suggestions might lead.

A particularly vicious spattering of rain against the window-pane roused the rector from his chair.

'I must be getting back,' he said, sighing. 'There was just one thing that I wanted to ask you – but I seem to have forgotten it.' He looked about the snug room, so different from his own bleak drawing-room which no amount of firing seemed to make habitable.

'Anything to do with committee work?' asked Harold Shoosmith resignedly. He was already a member of the Cricket Club, Football Club, British Legion, Parochial Church Council and the local branch of the R.S.P.C.A., after a residence of less than two months.

The rector's wrinkled brow became smooth again.

'How clever of you!' he cried. 'Yes, it was. The Thrush Green Entertainments Committee asked me to invite you to join them. We make most of the arrangements for our local activities. This business of the memorial will probably be dealt with by the T.G.E.C.'

Harold Shoosmith thought quickly. He felt as though the shade of Nathaniel Patten hovered anxiously at his elbow, pleading for justice and for mercy. If he accepted the committee's invitation, at least he would hold a watching brief for his long-dead friend and could do his best to see that his memorial would be a worthy one.

'I'd be very glad to join the committee,' said Harold honestly, as he opened the front door, and let out the rector into the inhospitable night.

'Very good of you indeed,' said the rector warmly. 'You will be more than welcome. The Entertainments Committee needs new blood. It does indeed!'

Beaming his farewells, the rector splashed bravely, in his wet shoes, towards the gate.

8. Sam Curdle is Observed

RAIN continued to sweep the Cotswolds throughout November and the wooded hills were shrouded in undulating grey veils. The fields of stubble, which had lain, bleached and glinting, under the kind October sun, were being slowly and patiently ploughed by panting tractors which traversed their length and turned over rib after rib of earth glistening like wet chocolate.

Young Doctor Lovell found his hands full. Coughs, colds, wheezy chests, ear-ache, rheumatic pains, stomachic chills and general depression kept his car splashing along the flooded lanes of Thrush Green and Lulling. In this, his first practice, he was a happy man. Thrush Green had brought him not only work, but also a wife, to love. The thought of their child, so soon to be born, gave him deep satisfaction. It was no wonder that Doctor Lovell whistled as blithely as a winter robin as he went about among his ailing patients. Some viewed his cheerfulness sourly.

'Proper heartless young fellow,' they grumbled, revelling in their own miseries.

But most of them were glad to greet a little brightness among the November gloom.

His senior partner in the practice, Doctor Bailey, did very little these days and found the weather particularly trying. Like most of Thrush Green's inhabitants he kept the fire company while the rain poured down.

Winnie, his wife, viewed his condition with secret alarm. He seemed to have difficulty with his breathing, and she did her best to persuade him to take a holiday abroad where they would find some sunshine.

'Can't be done, my dear,' wheezed the aged doctor. 'Costs

too much, for one thing, and young Lovell's got too much to do anyway. At least I can take surgery for him now and again. He'll need to feel free to go and see Ruth when the baby comes.'

He caught sight of the anxiety in his wife's face, and spoke cheerfully.

'Don't worry so. I've been fitter this year than I have for ages. It's just this dampness. It'll pass, I promise you.'

'You must take care, Donald. Keep in the warm and read – or better still, shall I see if Harold Shoosmith is free for a game of bridge this afternoon?'

The doctor's eye brightened. The newcomer to Thrush Green had many attributes which his neighbours approved. That of a fair-to-average bridge player made him particularly welcome in the Baileys' household.

'Good idea,' agreed Doctor Bailey, sounding more robust at once. 'And maybe Dimity and Ella will come as well.'

He watched his wife bustle from the room to the telephone and lay back, contentedly enough, in the deep armchair. He was more tired than he would admit to her. The thought of sunshine filled him with longings, but the effort of getting to it he knew was beyond his strength. Better to lie quietly at Thrush Green, letting the rainy days slip by, until the spring brought the benison of English sunlight and daffodils again.

The room was very quiet. The old man closed his eyes and listened to the small domestic noises around him. The fire whispered in the hearth, a log hissed softly as its moss-covered bark dried in the flames, and the doctor's ancient cat purred rustily in its throat. Somewhere outside, there was the distant sound of metal on stone as a workman repaired a gatepost. A child called, its voice high and tremulous like the bleating of a lamb, and a man answered it. Doctor Bailey felt a great peace enfolding him, and remembered a snatch of poetry from 'The

Task,' which he had learnt as a small boy almost seventy years ago.

> 'Stillness, accompanied with sounds so soft,
> Charms more than silence.'

He was blessed, he told himself, in having a retentive memory which tossed him such pleasures as this to enhance his daily round. He was blessed, too, with a wonderful wife and a host of good friends. Half-dozing now, he saw their faces float before him, friends of his boyhood, friends of his student days, friends among his patients. Most clearly of all he saw the face of the great Mrs Curdle whose burial he had attended at St Andrew's two years before. The flashing dark eyes, the imperiously jutting nose and the black plaited hair delighted his mind's eye as keenly as ever. He fancied himself again inside her caravan home, sipping the bitter brew of strong tea with which she always welcomed him. He saw again the dazzling stove which was her great pride, the swinging oil lamp, and the photograph of George, her much-loved son, whose birth might well have caused the death of his mother had young Doctor Bailey not acted promptly so many years ago. Bouquets of gaudy artificial flowers floated before the old man's closed eyes – each a tribute to his skill, a debt paid yearly by the magnificent gipsy woman he was proud to call his friend. Dear Mrs Curdle, whose annual fair had welcomed in each May at Thrush Green – there would never be another like her!

The door opened and his wife stood before him.

'They'll all come,' she said, smiling.

'Thank God for good friends,' said the doctor simply, turning from those in the shades to the living again.

If Harold Shoosmith was welcomed as a bridge player at the Baileys' he was just as warmly welcomed as a next-door neighbour by Miss Watson and Miss Fogerty at the village school.

It is essential for anyone in charge of children to have tolerant neighbours. The number of balls that fly over fences and have to be retrieved is prodigious. There are those who answer the timid knocking, rather low down, at the front door with an exasperated mien which strikes terror into the heart of the importuners. The newcomer was not one of these. Nor did he toss the balls back into the playground so that they rolled hither and thither to be picked up by any joyous passing hound.

If the children were at play he would hand their property to them with a smile. He went further. If he came across the bright balls in the grass or among his plants when school was over, he took the trouble to go round to Miss Watson's house and present them to her with the small old-fashioned bow and charming smile which caused so many female hearts to flutter at Thrush Green.

Miss Fogerty spent many evenings in Miss Watson's company these days, and it was natural that the two ladies should discuss the good fortune of having such a pleasant neighbour.

Miss Watson's sprained ankle still gave her pain although the stick had been discarded. On the few November evenings when the rain stopped, Miss Fogerty helped her friend to dig the flower border which ran along the communicating stone wall between the school garden and Harold Shoosmith's. After their labours they would retire into the school-house living-room and have a light meal of sandwiches and fruit.

Miss Fogerty relished these companionable hours. She had lived for years in her prim and somewhat dismal lodgings, with very few friends of her own. Miss Watson's invitations gave her great happiness, and the thought that her headmistress too might have felt the pangs of loneliness did not enter the modest little woman's head. She was glad to have been of use in a crisis and rejoiced now in the pleasure of Miss Watson's friendship.

Over the cheese sandwiches one evening Miss Watson spoke of yet another of their neighbour's kindnesses. It was a year when the apple crop had been a bumper one, and Harold Shoosmith, appalled at the thought of eating apples in some guise or the other for the rest of the year, had presented the schoolchildren with a sackful which stood at Miss Watson's back door.

'We are lucky to have him next door,' agreed Miss Fogerty.

'He must be missed by his firm,' continued Miss Watson, pouring coffee.

'With a firm?' echoed Miss Fogerty. 'I heard he had been in the Army.'

'And the Navy and Air Force,' said Miss Watson, a little tartly. 'People spread these rumours about in the most terrible way!' From her manner one might have thought that there was something shameful about all the Services.

'He very kindly gave me a lift up from Lulling the other day and talked about his work in Africa quite openly. I've no idea why people think he makes a mystery of his past, I'm sure.'

'He may have felt that he could confide in you,' suggested Miss Fogerty, her moist devoted eyes fixed upon her new friend. Miss Watson looked gratified.

'Well, I don't know about that—' she began in the sort of deprecating tone people use when they secretly agree with a statement made. 'But he certainly told me quite a bit about himself. He was with Sleepwell's for over thirty years, evidently. He was manager for all Africa – a most responsible position, I should think.'

'Sleepwell?' echoed Miss Fogerty in bewilderment. 'You mean the stuff you mix with hot milk?'

'Of course,' said Miss Watson. 'People need to sleep in Africa, I imagine, as well as in England.'

'But hot milk,' protested her friend. 'In Africa! It seems so wrong. Surely they would prefer fruit squash or something cooling.'

'I believe the nights are quite chilly,' said Miss Watson, with as much conviction as she could muster. She was a little shaky about the climatic conditions in the darkest continent and felt it would be as well to steer the conversation to surer ground.

'Anyway, Sleepwell seems to be a very popular drink there,' she continued, 'otherwise Mr Shoosmith wouldn't have stayed there for all that time.'

'Whereabouts in Africa was his business?' enquired Miss Fogerty. 'My cousin's family came from Nairobi. He may have met them.' She spoke as though Africa and Thrush Green were of approximately the same size.

'Somewhere on the west coast, I gather.' Miss Watson furrowed her brow. 'At a place with a name like Winnie Khaki. It's where Nathaniel Patten started his settlement, you know. He began with a little mission school for the native children, and now, Mr Shoosmith says, there's a village with a church, and school and a magnificent hospital.'

'It's strange to think,' said Miss Fogerty musingly, 'that Thrush Green sent Nathaniel Patten to Africa, and Nathaniel Patten has indirectly sent Mr Shoosmith back to Thrush Green.'

'And a very good thing for us that he did,' said her friend briskly, collecting the débris of their simple meal. 'He's a great asset to the place.'

Together they repaired to the kitchen sink to wash-up before Miss Fogerty made her way home to her lodgings.

To little Paul Young and his crony Christopher Mullins, Harold Shoosmith appeared in a different light. He was a man to be avoided, outwitted and feared. Needless to say, he had no idea of this.

The two boys had shifted their headquarters from the thinning greenery of the ox-eyed daisies to a tree on the side of Harold Shoosmith's spinney furthest from his house. This decrepit elm had been cut off some twelve feet above the ground in the early days of the Farmers' residence at the corner house. Half-hearted attempts had been made to remove the hollow stump, but it had defied its molesters and still stood firmly, overlooking the small grassy valley where Dotty Harmer lived.

Bushy young growth sprouted from its battered crown and concealed the boys from sight. They had cut rough footholds in the mouldering interior of the split trunk and could climb up easily enough to this exciting new hide-out. It was unlikely that the new tenant would discover them, and unlikely that he would seriously object even if he did so, but the two boys found it more thrilling to pretend that poor Harold Shoosmith was a monster, and persuaded themselves easily enough that he would shout, brandish a stick, report them to their parents, the police and their headmaster, with dire consequences, should he ever stumble upon their whereabouts on his premises. This, naturally, gave their meetings a delicious fillip.

One misty Saturday afternoon in November the two friends sat aloft in their eyrie, unknown, of course, to their parents.

'Chris Mullins has asked me to play,' Paul had said to his mother, and she, in her innocence, had imagined that he would be playing in the Mullins' garden.

'Paul Young's asked me to play with him,' Christopher had said to his mother, who had fondly thought that her son would be safely on the Youngs' premises.

By such simple strategy have boys, throughout the centuries, accomplished their nefarious ends.

Paul had arrived first and watched his friend emerge from the green garden door in the wall across the valley. He watched him run up the grassy hill and warbled an owl's cry as he approached. This was their secret sign, and the fact that an owl warbling in daylight might arouse suspicions, had not occurred to the boys.

Chris arrived quite breathless at the tree and Paul tugged him up the rough stairway joyously.

'I've brought a Mars bar and some transfers,' he announced proudly when his friend had found a precarious seat.

'I've only got two apples,' confessed Chris. 'It's all we seem to have in our house,' he continued bitterly. 'Apples, apples, apples!'

Paul sympathised. There is a limit to the number of apples even a small boy can eat. This year's crop was proving an embarrassment.

'My mum,' went on Christopher, 'says that they clean your teeth, and chocolate ruins them. Been reading something in the papers, I expect.' He spoke with disgust. Paul found such contempt of parents wholly wonderful, and broke the Mars bar carefully in half. A few delicious damp crumbs fell upon the leg of his corduroy trousers and he licked them up thoughtfully, running his finger-nail down the grooves afterwards to collect any stray morsels which might have become embedded there. They munched in amicable silence. From their perch they commanded an extensive view. Far to the west Paul could see a white ground mist veiling the lower part of a distant hollow. Only the tips of the bushy scrub protruded from the drowned field – like rabbits' ears, thought Paul idly – and he watched a distant hedge becoming more and more ghostly as the mist wreathed and swirled through it. As yet their own little valley had but a slight mistiness, but it was obvious that fog would engulf all by nightfall.

'Let's see your transfers,' said Christopher, wiping his sticky hands down his trousers perfunctorily. Paul fished in his pocket and handed over a crumpled booklet. He watched his friend anxiously. Would he think they were babyish? Some of the transfers were of toys – a ball, a kite and a doll. He could not bear to be ridiculed by his idol.

To his relief Chris seemed pleased with what he saw. He tore out a Union Jack, placed it carefully face downward on the back of his hand and licked it heavily with a tongue still dusky with chocolate. Paul chose a picture of a football boot – it seemed a manly choice – and licked as heartily.

'Seen old Shoelace?' asked Chris as they waited for the transfers to work. This nickname was considered by both boys to be the height of humour.

'Not a sign,' said Paul. 'Must be out, I think.' Even as he spoke there was a cracking of twigs on the other side of the spinney.

'Get down!' whispered Chris urgently. The two boys cowered low among the scanty brushwood. Paul could hear his heart beating under the green jersey Aunt Ruth had knitted him. His nose was so close to the transfer on his hand that he could smell the oily pungency from it. The silence became unendurable. Suddenly a blackbird chattered loudly and flew from the little wood. Silence fell again, and after a few more breathless minutes the boys straightened up.

'Gosh!' breathed Chris, 'I thought we'd been found that time.' They sat listening intently for a few more minutes, and then Paul sighed with relief.

'No one there, Chris. Let's peel off our transfers. You first.'

'No, you first,' said Christopher, punching his friend affectionately on the arm. 'Mine'll take longer to do with all the lines on the flag.'

'What about all the twiddly bits on my boot?' objected

Paul. 'All right, all right,' he added hastily, as his friend's fist was raised again. 'I'll do mine first.'

Carefully he raised the corner of his damp transfer. His tongue protruded with the effort as he began to peel it gently away from his pink hand. Half-way across the picture began to disintegrate.

'Press it back again quick,' urged Christopher. 'And huff on the back. You ought always to huff on transfers. The wet in your breath keeps it the right temperature.' He watched anxiously as Paul obeyed.

They rested their hands on their knees and breathed energetically upon the back of the transfers. Paul tried again, gingerly peeling the damp paper away. He was rewarded by an almost perfect picture of the football boot.

'Only one of the laces a bit wonky,' he said proudly. 'Not bad, is it?' He held up his hand for Chris to admire, but his friend was much too busy revealing his own masterpiece. The result was disappointing. Only half the Union Jack adhered to Christopher's hand.

Paul tried not to look too smug. Christopher he knew, liked to excel at everything, and could be violent when things went wrong.

'D'you know why mine didn't take?' demanded Chris belligerently. 'I'll tell you,' he continued, without giving his apprehensive friend time to answer. 'It's because I'm so much *stronger* than you are! That's why!' He thrust an aggressive face towards Paul's.

'Stronger?' faltered the smaller boy.

'Yes,' said Christopher. 'See the back of my hand? Smothered in hairs, isn't it?' He held up his grubby paw, and against the light, one or two faint hairs were discernible. 'That shows I'm strong. Like Samson, remember? Well, transfers won't take on a hairy hand, naturally. You have to have sissy smooth hands

like yours for transfers to work. It's a kid's game, anyway.' He tossed the book back to Paul who put it silently back in his pocket. The afternoon was not going as it should, and Paul began to wonder how he could put matters right.

It was at this uncomfortable moment that they saw the man.

He came into their line of vision as he swung down the hill towards Dotty Harmer's garden. He had evidently come from the lane that led to Nod and Nidden from Thrush Green, and he was about two hundred yards from the tree where the boys watched him.

He reached the low gate in Dotty's hedge, leant upon it and looked around him. Apart from Dotty's cottage no other house looked out upon this little valley. Harold Shoosmith's view was obscured by the projecting curve of the spinney, and, as far as the man could see, he was unobserved. He opened the gate, walked to the hen-house and disappeared inside.

There was no movement from the house as the cackling of

hens made itself heard. In fact, Dotty was busy shopping in Lulling at that moment, and the house was deserted except for Mrs Curdle, Dotty's black cat.

Within a few minutes the man emerged carrying a brown-paper carrier bag. He latched the hen-house door, and departed up the hill again with swift easy strides. The boys could see his face quite clearly as he vanished over the brow of the hill towards the lane.

'That was Sam Curdle,' said Paul. 'Do you reckon he was taking things? Eggs, say, or even a chicken?' He looked rather shocked and alarmed. Christopher, who did not know the history of the Curdle family as well as his friend did, was less impressed.

'He didn't look as though he was doing anything wrong. P'raps someone asked him to feed the chickens for them.'

'Might have,' admitted Paul doubtfully. 'But he's an awful thief, Chris. Everybody says so. D'you reckon we ought to tell somebody?'

'If we do,' pointed out Chris, 'they'll ask us what we were doing here, and that's the end of the camp for us.'

'I hadn't thought of that,' confessed Paul unhappily. They sat in silence for some time turning the problem over in their minds. Paul felt sure that Sam had been up to no good; but Chris was right in saying that they could not afford to disclose what they had seen. Of course, Paul told himself, Dotty might have asked Sam to look at her chickens, as Chris had said. It might all have been above-board. He hoped it was – more for the sake of keeping their hiding place secret than from anxiety on Dotty's behalf.

But he was far from happy about the matter. He watched the white mist thickening in the distant hollow and saw that it was beginning to seep along towards their own valley. Suddenly the afternoon seemed chilly and wretched. Everything had been horrid. The transfers had failed, Chris had hit him far harder than was necessary for real friendship, he felt slightly sick with too much chocolate, and sicker still at the thought of keeping all he had seen a guilty secret from his mother.

All at once he wanted to be at home with her – to be warm and dry, to see the fire dancing and to hear his parents talking. A great distaste for the camp, for old Shoelace, and for the wet mustiness of the decaying tree suddenly suffused the boy.

'I'm going home,' he said abruptly, and slithered rapidly to the ground.

Chris, astonished and silent, followed him.

'See you Monday,' said Paul shortly, setting off for home on the west side of the copse. Without answering, Christopher plunged down the hill in the opposite direction through the thickening mist. As he ran he became conscious of a stickiness on the back of his hand. Exasperatedly he clawed the remains of the unsuccessful transfer from it with his finger-nail.

Altogether, he thought bitterly, it had been a beast of an afternoon.

As the melancholy month of November wore on Dimity and Ella found themselves getting to know the newcomer quite well. As well as meeting him at the occasional bridge party, and coming across him on their walks abroad, the rector, who had always been a frequent visitor to their cottage, now often came accompanied by his new friend.

Both ladies were delighted. As Ella said, there were far too few unattached men about Thrush Green and their company was quite refreshing after all their single women friends.

Harold Shoosmith went at first with some reluctance to the cottage, but had been pressed to do so when returning with the rector from a country walk on one or two occasions. He was welcomed so warmly that his shyness deserted him. He found too that the two women held an attraction for him. He was sorry for Dimity, considering her outrageously treated by her domineering friend. It needed the rector's wise words to point out that Dimity's life of service was also her crown of glory, and that she was completely happy.

Harold Shoosmith's feelings towards Ella were mixed. Her outspokenness half-shocked and half-amused him. Her physical clumsiness revolted him. Her generosity and warm-heartedness compelled his admiration. But overriding all these feelings was one of fascinated horror at her artistic creations. He was a man who liked recognisable patterns. His shirts were striped or checked. His ties were plain, striped or of a traditional paisley design. His curtains carried fleurs-de-lis and his chair-covers matched them.

Ella's strong blobs of colour, irregularly placed on a background of nobbly black broken checks, appalled his sense of order. The very idea of letting her loose on the memorial to Nathaniel made him quake.

It was this preoccupation with the possibility that led Harold Shoosmith to visit the cottage so often. So far he had heard no more about Ella's part in the project. A meeting had been held in the school to see what Thrush Green felt about the plan. Wholeheartedly the inhabitants had agreed to mark the occasion of Nathaniel's centenary with a suitable memorial. They had, furthermore, voted that the proceeds of that year's Fur and Feather Whist Drive be devoted to the fund. The rector had then exhorted them to go home to put their minds to work on the best type of memorial to their greatest son, and to put their suggestions in the box provided in the church porch. Another meeting to vote on the results was to be held early in December.

Harold Shoosmith found the suspense almost unbearable. The two ladies never spoke about it, and he found that he could not bring himself to broach so painful a subject. He comforted himself with the thought that Ella must surely have mentioned the matter if she had been approached. It was too much to expect that such a forthright person would be so delicately reticent.

Meanwhile he made a point of being particularly kind to timid little Dimity. His attentions were much appreciated by that modest lady and did not go unnoticed by Ella Bembridge – nor, for that matter, by the good rector.

Even sour old Mr Piggott felt a certain warmth towards Thrush Green's latest resident, for he was the means by which the sexton resumed his role of detective.

On the last day of the month he went to the corner house to cut back the laurel hedge that grew just inside the communicating wall between the school-house garden and Harold Shoosmith's.

He slashed lustily with a small bill-hook, for the laurels were grossly overgrown. The glossy green leaves fluttered to the ground around him. After one particularly vicious onslaught a small object, which had lodged in a crook of a bough, fell at his feet. Bending painfully, old Piggott retrieved it and held it up in the waning light.

Joy coursed its unaccustomed way through his hardening veins. It was a wallet – and without a doubt it was the one which Miss Watson had lost on the night of the burglary. It was empty, but that was only to be expected.

'The first clue!' chortled old Piggott, pocketing it carefully. 'I'll get 'im yet!'

And, much encouraged, he bent to his task again.

PART TWO

Christmas at Thrush Green

9. The Memorial

THE meeting to decide upon Nathaniel Patten's memorial was well attended. The infants' room at the village school was almost uncomfortably full. Small thin people squeezed into the desks at one side of the room, and the more portly sat sedately on the desks themselves or on the few low tables upon which the babies usually pursued their activities. A pile of minute bentwood armchairs remained stacked in the corner, for not even Dimity could have folded her small stature into such a confined space.

The rector sat at Miss Fogerty's desk as he was chairman. Harold Shoosmith found himself sharing a desk top with Ella and wondered, somewhat unchivalrously if it would bear their combined weight.

As the latecomers drifted in, to prop themselves against the partition or the ancient piano, Harold gazed idly at the notices pinned to the wall. They were written in large black letters and were obviously the work of Miss Fogerty. 'MY BIRTHDAY,' said one, 'IS TODAY.' Below this dramatic announcement two names, Anne and John, had been inserted into a slot provided for the purpose.

'MONITORS THIS WEEK,' said another, 'John, Elizabeth, Anne.'

'WE FORGOT OUR HANDKERCHIEFS,' the third confessed frankly. Only John appeared to be culpable.

'That chap John seems to lead an active life,' observed Harold to Ella. 'And Anne for that matter,' he added.

'They're all called Anne or John,' explained Ella kindly. 'Unless they're Amanda or Roxana or Jacqueline or Marilyn or Somesuch.'

'I see,' said Harold, light dawning. 'Seems a pity the old names aren't used,' he mused. 'My sisters had friends with good old names like Bertha and Gertrude.' He paused, and appeared to rack his brain for more, but failed to add to the list. 'What's wrong with Bertha and Gertrude?' he added rhetorically of his neighbour.

'Plenty,' said Ella simply.

At this point the rector banged the desk with Miss Fogerty's safety inkwell and the meeting began.

'I must thank you for the excellent suggestions which have been put into the box,' began the rector. 'We have had five put forward – well, four, really, I suppose. I'll just read them out and if there are any more ideas we can then add them to the list.'

He adjusted a pair of half-glasses upon his snub nose and peered at the back of *The Quarterly Letter to Incumbents* upon which he had written his notes. The glasses gave his chubby face an oddly Pickwickian look. His hearers watched him with affection.

'What about putting up the suggestions on the blackboard?' suggested a bright youth perched on the nature table beside the winter berries.

'An excellent notion,' agreed the rector. Miss Fogerty hurried forward from the side of the piano.

'Oh, do let me put it up for you,' she fluttered, beginning to tug the easel from its nightly resting place against a map of the Holy Land.

Harold Shoosmith and the bright youth politely disengaged Miss Fogerty from the unequal struggle and she returned, pink with pleasure, to her place by the piano to watch the men's efforts with the board pegs.

'If I might suggest—' she began timidly, as the youth exerted all his pressure upon a peg too large for the hole, 'the one *above* is easier.'

The board leant at a drunken angle as the boy adjusted the awkward peg. He and Harold hoisted it one jump higher and stood back to admire their handiwork. Miss Fogerty's neat printing told a simple but poignant tale upon the blackboard's face.

NED IS IN BED
HIS LEG IS BAD
NED'S PET TED BIT NED'S LEG.
BAD TED TO BITE NED'S LEG!

All eyes were riveted upon the board with an attention which must have warmed Miss Fogerty's heart had she been less flustered. One or two enchanted members of her elderly class read the words aloud with slow absorption.

The rector, seeing his parishioners' attention deflected so wholeheartedly, sighed resignedly and took off his spectacles, preparing to wait.

'There's a case in point,' observed Harold to Ella. 'Ned! You simply never hear of a Ned these days.' He scrutinised the blackboard carefully.

'Or Ted, even. Used to be dozens of Teds when I was a boy. Proper names, I mean, not hooligans.'

Ella did not reply as she was trying to attract Dimity's attention. Dimity had found a resting place on a low table beneath the window and was idly unscrewing the bone acorn attached to the window blind.

The rector coughed apologetically and called his wayward flock to the business in hand.

'May we rub out your lesson, Miss Fogerty?' he enquired kindly.

'Oh, yes, indeed. Please do,' quavered the lady. The bright youth eagerly accepted the proffered blackboard cleaner and dashed away at the writing amidst clouds of chalk and general regret.

'The first suggestion,' said the rector resuming his glasses, 'is a sundial.'

'Shall I put it up?' asked the boy, fingering a lovely long stick of chalk handed to him from Miss Fogerty's store.

'If you please,' said the rector.

Rather crookedly the word was written in a passable copper plate. As an afterthought, the boy added the figure 1 in front of it.

'Secondly,' said the rector, 'a fountain. I suppose that means a drinking fountain,' he added doubtfully.

'Not at all,' said the oldest Miss Lovelock. 'I envisaged plumes of water flashing in the sunlight. Like Versailles, you know.'

'I see,' said the rector gravely.

'Be the devil of a job laying the water across the green,' observed someone in the front row.

'Remember them a-laying of them electric light wires?' reminisced his neighbour. 'Cor! That were a proper Fred Karno affair, that were! Best part of the summer—'

'*Please*!' said the rector beseechingly. 'We must get on. Discussion later, please.'

There were apologetic growlings and the vicar consulted his list again.

'A Celtic cross comes next.'

'Celtic!' burst out Ella, in a booming voice that set a wire humming inside the decrepit piano. 'Why Celtic? What's wrong with a decent plain *English* cross for Thrush Green? Too much altogether of this twilight-of-the-gods and Deirdre-of-the-sorrows nonsense!'

The rector turned a look more anguished than angered upon her, and Ella subsided with a gruff 'Sorry!'

'How do you spell "Celtic?" ' asked the boy at the blackboard, waggling the chalk in hesitant fingers.

Several people told him several versions. More by luck than judgement an accepted spelling was finally inscribed, with a neat 3 in front.

'There were a number of slips of paper,' continued the rector, 'bearing the suggestion that a statue of Nathaniel Patten should be erected.'

A warm buzz went round the room. It was obvious that this idea was most welcome.

'Statue,' said the youth, pressing unduly upon the chalk and snapping it in two. His finger-nails scratched the board and there was a hissing as several people drew in their breath sharply.

'Puts your teeth on edge, don't it?' said old Mr Piggott glumly.

'Not so bad as a slate pencil,' said his elderly neighbour.

'Ah! It's walking on a stone floor in me socks that touches me up,' said someone else conversationally. 'Specially if your feet's a bit damp-like. Fair turns your teeth to chalk that does.'

'Sorry all,' said the boy cheerfully, diving to retrieve one of the pieces from under the pedal of the piano. The rector, seeing his meeting stray once again, rapped smartly with the inkwell once more.

'There are several modifications of this last suggestion,' he said in a firm voice, looking severely over his half glasses at old Piggott who was embarking upon a long rigmarole about the reaction of false as against natural teeth when they were being set on edge. Reluctantly Piggott rumbled to a halt.

'Some have put "life-size," some have said the kind of material they prefer, such as "bronze" or "stone," and one rather charming suggestion wonders if Nathaniel might be surrounded by a group of African children for whom he did so much.' The rector's kindly gaze seemed to stray towards Dimity who twisted the acorn with such agitation that it fell off and rolled under a radiator.

'Let me,' said Harold Shoosmith, kneeling down with an alacrity and suppleness which the rector envied. Not even a knee-crack, noted the rector wistfully, remembering the reports, which habitually punctuated the services, from his own stiffening joints.

The acorn had rolled as far as it could into the murk under the radiator. Harold lay down at full-length and pulled out a toffee paper, part of a jig-saw puzzle, a rusty drawing-pin, two beads and a handful of grey fluff.

'Really!' said Miss Watson, turning pink. 'I must speak to the cleaner.' She looked most annoyed. She had not been too pleased to see Miss Fogerty's archaic reading lesson made so public. There were plenty of bright modern readers in the cupboards, specially recommended by the new infants' school adviser for the area. It gave such a wrong impression to see all that stuff about Ned's bad leg on the board. Fond as she was of dear Agnes there was no doubt about it she was just a shade behind the times. And now all this rubbish being brought to light! Really teachers had enough, one way or another, to drive them quite mad, thought poor mortified Miss Watson, tugging at her cardigan.

Harold retrieved the acorn and scrambled nimbly to his feet, smiling at Dimity. The rector, collecting his wits, returned to the fray.

'Are there any more suggestions?' he asked. The heavy silence which met this remark was only to be expected. People lowered their eyes to inspect the desk lids or their own shoes. Somebody blew his nose like a trumpet, and the boy by the blackboard, who had been studying his broken finger-nail with close interest, now bit it off briskly with a decisive snap.

'Well, shall we take the suggestions in turn?' asked the rector. 'How do we feel about the sundial?'

'Not bad,' said Edward Young cautiously. 'It would look rather well on the green, I think.'

Eyes were turned respectfully on the young architect. After all, he should know something about these things with all those years of training behind him.

Doctor Bailey rose to his feet from a desk at the back.

'It was my suggestion. I felt it wouldn't be too expensive, nor too big – I can't help feeling that a statue might dominate our small green rather too much – and might be useful too.'

'Thank you,' said the rector. 'Any comments?'

'Well, we've got a clock on the church already,' pointed out old Piggott sourly. 'And that tells the time fair enough, rain or shine, which is more'n you can say for a sundial.'

'True,' agreed the doctor equably. There was a long pause broken at last by the rector.

'Shall we go on to the next item? The fountain?'

'Wouldn't never work,' said someone dourly.

'Get frozen up come winter,' said another heavily.

'All the kids would come home sopping wet,' came a woman's voice from the back. 'Might even get drowned. You know what kids are!'

Murmurs of gloomy assent greeted this cheerful remark. The rector looked apologetically at the oldest Miss Lovelock, who continued to smile and nod her trembling head with unconcern.

No further comments being made the rector consulted his list again.

'Now we come to the Celtic cross,' said he.

'Well, you know my feelings on *that*,' boomed Ella heartily.

She hoisted her bulk round to face the assembly. 'Whose idea was it anyway?' she asked forthrightly.

There was no reply to her belligerent question. Harold Shoosmith, half appalled and half amused, could not help feeling that it would be a brave man indeed who admitted to such folly before that stalwart Amazon. As a matter of fact, it had been Ruth Lovell's innocent suggestion, but although Edward Young, her brother-in-law, knew this, he kept silence. Ruth, at home on the sofa, at that moment enduring the belabourings of her unborn babe, would have been amused at the scene.

'Then I take it there are no further points?' queried the rector, hurrying to safer ground. 'And that brings us to the statue.'

Released from the tension of Ella's making, tongues now began to wag more readily.

'That's the best idea of the lot,' said one.

'The *only* thing,' said another downrightly.

'A real good big 'un,' suggested another. 'Don't want nothin' mean-lookin'!'

There was quite a hubbub in the little room and the rector was forced to thump again with the red inkwell.

'I really think the time has come to take a vote on these suggestions,' he said. 'Shall we raise hands? Those in favour of the statue?'

Almost all the hands in the room seemed to be aloft. The rector stood up, the better to do his counting, then turned to Harold.

'Shoosmith, my dear fellow, would you check for me?'

The two men stood at the front of the classroom on tiptoe, their mouths slightly open, their foreheads slightly wrinkled in concentration. On the wall the great clock ticked in the sudden quietness, and outside in the wet December night a distant car splashed along the muddy lane to Nod and Nidden.

'Thirty-seven,' said Harold Shoosmith.

'Thirty-seven,' agreed the rector. 'I think there's no doubt that the statue will be our choice, but it would be wise to vote upon the others in turn. Now, first of all, the sundial!'

A few hands went up, including Edward Young's.

'Seven,' said Harold.

'Eight,' said the rector.

'Sorry,' said the bright youth who had perched himself again on the nature table. 'I was scratching under my arm.'

'Seven it is then,' said the rector. 'Now the fountain!'

Only three hands were raised in support of Miss Lovelock's suggestion. The delights of the flashing plumes in summer sunlight were obviously overborne by the thought of the trench-digging and freezing possibilities put forward by the killjoys earlier.

The Celtic cross fared even worse, whether by reason of Ella's contumely, natural patriotic pride, or plain apathy, no one could tell, but only two hands were raised aloft, one of them belonging to the nail-biting boy.

'Well,' said the rector. 'That seems to be that.'

An excited buzz ran round the room. There seemed to be general pleasure at the verdict. Above the hum the sound of St Andrew's church clock could be heard, striking eight.

The rector rapped again, after looking at Harold Shoosmith and Edward Young.

'Perhaps while we are all here together we might go a little further into this question of the statue.'

'Time's getting on,' said the woman at the back. 'My husband wants to get down to "The Two Pheasants," but he's minding the baby.'

'Do him good,' said Ella robustly. 'Don't you hurry back.'

There was general laughter.

'Ah maybe!' replied the woman grudgingly. ' 'Tis all

right for you single 'uns to talk, but us poor married toads has to keep the boat up straight!'

'It does seem,' said the rector, ignoring the interruption and secretly fearful of being drawn into this incipient argument, 'that there are a number of points to bear in mind. First of all, I think Mr Young will tell us, a life-size statue of Nathaniel Patten will be an expensive affair. Not only are there the materials to pay for, but the sculptor too.'

'I don't see why Miss Bembridge can't be given a chance,' said someone at the back. 'We'd all be proud to see her work on our green.'

'Good Lord!' exclaimed Ella. 'I've never done anything like that!' Her eye began to gleam with a dangerously creative light. 'But I wouldn't mind having a bash,' she added, with growing enthusiasm.

Harold Shoosmith trembled. He had settled himself beside Dimity, after screwing back the acorn, and she looked at him with sudden anxiety as their shared table-top shook.

The rector, with an aplomb born of many similar village crises, spoke smoothly.

'I'm sure we can come to some arrangement later about the person we ask to undertake the work, but first of all I think we should decide what medium we want. Bronze has been suggested or stone of some sort.'

'A nice bit of pink granite,' suggested old Piggott, 'well shone up.'

Edward Young shuddered.

'I like copper myself,' said his neighbour. 'Goes that nice green shade in time.'

'We'd get it pinched,' commented the bright boy. 'Copper fetches ten bob a lump these days. A *small* lump. Come to that, any sort of metal statue's going to cost a packet. Specially life-size.'

This sound piece of sense brought forth a few grunts of agreement, and a small speech from Dimity.

'In this connection, perhaps I could withdraw my first suggestion about a group of figures,' she began breathlessly, her earnest gaze fixed upon the rector's encouraging face. 'It did seem to me that *children* should be part of the memorial, but why not have *Nathaniel* as a child? After all, he played on the green as a little boy, and the statue would be much smaller and less expensive.'

'It's a very sensible and charming idea,' agreed the rector gently. Taking heart from his support, Dimity continued rather breathlessly.

'And it could be *most attractive*. I mean, look at Peter Pan! What could be sweeter? Perhaps the same person would do it?'

Edward Young opened his mouth as though to speak, thought better of it, and subsided.

'We will certainly bear that in mind, Miss Dean,' nodded the rector, watching Dimity resume her place beside Harold.

'Then we must choose our sculptor,' went on Mr. Henstock, 'one who can work in the medium of our choice, and give us a memorial which suits its surroundings and which we all are proud of.'

His plump face began to pucker with worry.

'It occurs to me that we must, of course, get planning permission from several authorities if we want to put up the statue. Really, there is a great deal to consider.'

Edward Young then spoke up.

'Perhaps you would allow me to make enquiries about prices and possible sculptors on behalf of us all here? I should be delighted to be of some service, and I think I could advise you too about the best way of approaching the necessary authorities.'

A hum of agreement ran round the room. The rector looked mightily relieved.

'It is most kind of you. Would someone propose that Mr Young should undertake this particular set of enquiries?'

'I will,' said Miss Watson briskly.

'And I'll second it,' added Doctor Bailey.

'That really is a great comfort,' said Mr Henstock gratefully. 'I am sure we are all much indebted to you for offering your professional help so freely.'

He turned over *The Quarterly Letter to Incumbents* and scrutinised it closely.

'Just one more thing,' he continued, looking at the assembled company over his glasses. 'A good friend of Thrush Green, who wishes to remain anonymous, has said that he would like to defray half the expense of this project. I think you might like to register your approval of this most generous offer.'

Loud clapping and a few foot-drummings demonstrated the fervour with which this announcement was met. As it died down, Edward Young spoke again.

'That is wonderful news, sir. I just wondered if it might not be a good idea to form a very small committee, representing all assembled here tonight, to go further into this statue business. For one thing, we shall want it unveiled presumably on Nathaniel's birthday, some time in March, I believe.'

'That's right,' said Harold. 'The fifteenth!'

'Then in that case, we must work quickly,' went on Edward. 'It might be rather nice if one of Nathaniel's descendants could unveil his memorial.'

'His daughter's dead,' said a very old man, who was leaning against Miss Fogerty's weather chart and smearing the black umbrellas and yellow suns most carelessly. 'Died soon after she were married. I knows that 'cos my sister and she used to send each other Christmas cards for years. There were a boy though, I do recollect.'

'That's most interesting,' said Mr Henstock. 'We'll follow

that up. Now, what about Mr Young's very sound suggestion? Shall we appoint someone – or two perhaps – to help him?'

'Yourself, sir,' suggested the bright boy.

There was a murmur of agreement.

'I shall be most happy,' said the rector. 'Doctor Bailey, do you feel that you could join Mr Young and me?'

Doctor Bailey shook his silvery head.

'I'd rather someone else took it on, if you don't mind. I'm not as reliable these days as I'd like to be. What about Mr Shoosmith?'

The name brought forth such a burst of warm assent that the normally self-possessed newcomer looked almost shy.

'I should be very glad to be of any use,' said Harold politely.

And so it was left. The three men would look further into the matter and let Thrush Green know more about their findings later.

It was almost nine o'clock when the company dispersed into the wet darkness.

'Keeps mild, don't it,' said the old man, who remembered Nathaniel's daughter, to Mr Piggott as they made their way to the brightly-lit pub.

'Ah!' responded old Piggott morosely. 'You know what they say about a green Christmas? Makes a full churchyard. And that makes more work for me, I may say.'

'I don't know as I believes that,' replied the old man with a flash of spirit, 'but that's as may be. What I do know is these meetings give a chap a rare thirst. You come on in and have a pint with me, my boy.'

At this generous invitation old Piggott's face softened a little, and united in a common bond, the two crossed the welcoming threshold of 'The Two Pheasants' and left the dark behind them.

10. Albert Piggott is Wooed

Nelly Tilling kept her word. She paid three visits to Mr Piggott's cottage, carrying with her each time a stout rush basket bearing a scrubbing brush, house flannel, and a large packet of detergent whose magic properties had been dinned into her by television advertisements. Nelly was a firm believer in the educational value of television, and took everything she saw as gospel truth.

Her set was an old one, given her by the landlord of 'The Drovers' Arms,' not far from her own cottage, where she worked two mornings a week scrubbing out the bar. Kindly Ted and Bessie Allen, for whom young Molly Piggott had once worked, felt very sorry for Nelly Tilling when her husband died and had decided that their old television set would be just the thing to cheer her lonely evenings.

They were quite right. Nelly was an avid watcher and took great delight in telling her employers all about the programmes – which they had seen for themselves the night before – in meticulous detail.

One morning, soon after the meeting about the memorial, Nelly made her way round to Mr Piggott's back door, her basket on her arm and her spirits raised at the thought of the work before her. Nelly was a fighter. She chased dirt as she chased and routed any weakness for strong drink or dubious entertainment. Brought up by militant evangelistic parents Nelly continued, in ripe middle age, to practise those precepts learnt in her youth. She knew where to draw the line, and even switched off the television set if any of the dancers appeared too lightly clad for her sense of propriety.

She intended this morning to attack Albert Piggott's kitchen. This task would have daunted many a woman, but

Nelly, armed with the magic detergent and the stout scrubbing brush, really looked forward to the job.

She found Albert Piggott gazing intently into a small triangle of looking-glass propped on the window-sill. He greeted her glumly.

'Got summat in me eye,' he said.

'Here, let's see,' said the fat widow, putting her heavy basket on the floor and advancing upon him. Albert turned a watery pale blue eye in her direction.

'That reminds me,' said the lady, pulling her handkerchief from her coat pocket and screwing the corner into a workman-like radish, 'I've brought a cod's head for your cat.'

Mr Piggott grunted, by way of thanking her, and looked with alarm at the handkerchief.

'It'll come out on its own, I don't doubt—' he began. But his protests were of no avail. He found the back of his head held firmly in Nelly Tilling's left hand while she swiped shrewdly at his eye with the formidable weapon in her right one.

Nelly Tilling had plenty of experience in dealing with refractory children. She had brought up three of her own, all scrubbed and polished like bright apples, and had the knack of grabbing a reluctant child behind the neck and whisking a soapy flannel round its face and ears before it had time to protest. Although all her children were now grown up, Nelly's hand had not lost its cunning. Within two seconds Albert was released, and the eye was freed of its foreign body.

'Well!' gasped Albert, flabbergasted but impressed. 'That was a smart piece of work, I will say!'

' 'Twas nothing,' said the widow, looking gratified nevertheless. 'While you're over the church, Albert, I thought I'd set this room to rights today, and maybe we could share a bacon pie, like I promised. I've got it in my basket here. I'll just hot it up for midday.'

Albert's eye brightened. For all her running him round, which he was inclined to resent, a bacon pie was a bacon pie, particularly when such a delicacy was virtually unobtainable to a man living alone.

'I'll pick a bit of winter green,' said Albert, with unaccustomed vigour, 'it's doing well this year. Give us the enamel bowl, my girl, and I'll go down the garden.'

He departed, whistling through his broken teeth, and Nelly set about heating some water for her campaign, well pleased with the way things were going.

Two hours later Nelly sat, blown but triumphant, on the kitchen chair and surveyed her handiwork.

She had cause for pride. A bright fire glowed behind gleaming bars, and the bacon pie was already in the oven beside it and beginning to smell most savoury. The thin little cat, her repast spread on a newspaper in the corner, dug her sharp white teeth into the cod's head, closing her eyes in bliss the while.

The floor, the walls and the wooden table had all been lustily scrubbed. Albert's dingy sink had been scoured to its original yellow colour, and the window above it gleamed and winked with unaccustomed cleanliness.

Taking a steady look at it, thought Nelly to herself, easing off her shoes for greater comfort, it wasn't such a bad little house, and certainly very much more conveniently placed for shopping than her own cottage at Lulling Woods.

Two rooms up and two rooms down would be just a nice size for Albert and herself, and her own furniture would look very handsome in these surroundings. The few poor sticks that Albert had collected over the years were fit for nothing but firewood.

She allowed her mind to dwell for a minute on her old schoolfellow in the role of husband. True, he was no oil painting, but she had long passed the age of needing good looks about her, and anyway, she admitted to herself with disarming frankness, her own beauty had long since gone.

And, of course, he was a miserable worm. But, Nelly pointed out to herself, he had some justification for it. The drink had something to do with it, no doubt, but lack of a decent woman in his house was the real cause of the trouble. She cast an appraising eye over the clean kitchen and listened to the music of the sizzling pie. With a cheerful place like this to come home to, thought Nelly, 'The Two Pheasants' would lose its appeal. And if by any chance it didn't, then Nelly Tilling would put her foot down – for hadn't she seen, with her own eyes, young Albert Piggott in a Norfolk jacket much too small for him, signing the pledge all those years ago?

The advantages of the marriage were solid ones. Albert

earned a steady wage, was a good gardener and could afford to keep a wife in reasonable comfort. There would be no need for her to go out to work. 'The Drovers' Arms' was a pleasant enough place to scrub out, but Nelly disliked seeing people drinking. She would not be sorry to give up the job there, despite Bessie and Ted's goodwill towards her.

At Thrush Green she would be able to pick and choose her employers. Miss Ruth or Miss Joan, as she still thought of Mrs Lovell and Mrs Young, could probably do with a hand. She remembered the great flagged kitchen floor at the Bassetts' house and her heart warmed.

Or better still, there was the village school practically next door! The thought of those yards of bare floorboards, pounded day in and day out by scores of muddy boots, fairly crying out for a bucket of hot suds and a good brush, filled Nelly's heart with joy. There was a cloakroom too, if she remembered rightly, with a nice rosy brick floor that really paid for doing. And there was something about a large tortoise stove, freshly done with first-class blacklead and plenty of elbow-grease, that gladdened your eyes. She had heard that Miss Watson wasn't best pleased with the present cleaner. A word dropped in the right ear, Nelly told herself, might bring her the job if she decided to earn an honest penny at Thrush Green.

She heard the sound of Albert's footsteps approaching, heaved her bulk from the chair, and opened the oven door. A glorious fragrance filled the room. On top of the hob the winter greens bubbled deliciously. The mingled scents greeted Albert as he opened the back door.

'Cor!' breathed Mr Piggott with awe, 'that smells wholly good, Nell.'

His face bore an expression of holiness and rapture which his habitual place of worship never saw. Albert was touched to his very marrow.

Nelly was not slow to follow up this advantage.

'Sit you down, Albert,' she said warmly, 'in a real clean kitchen at last, with a real hot meal to eat.'

She withdrew the fragrant dish from the oven, and put it, still sizzling, before the bedazzled sexton.

'There!' breathed the widow proudly, setting about her wooing with a bacon pie.

Albert Piggott's cottage was not the only house in Thrush Green where thoughts of matrimony disturbed the air.

On the same day, across the green, Ella Bembridge mused upon the married state. She was alone in the house, her work materials spread out upon the kitchen table. She was busy hand printing a length of material for Dotty Harmer's new summer skirt, and for once the dishes of paint, the jar of brushes and the chunky wood block failed to please her.

Dimity was out with Harold Shoosmith in the large Daimler. She would be more than adequately chaperoned, for about six cars were with them. The Lulling Field Club was off to see a Saxon church, much prized by antiquarians, resembling a stone bees' skep, and smelling strongly of damp. Ella had decided to forgo this pleasure and to get on with one or two orders while the kitchen was unoccupied.

But her heart was not in the work. The possibility of either of them marrying had been thought of when the two friends had joined forces many years before. As they grew older there was, naturally, less likelihood of marriage, and their lives had been filled with many interests and a cheerful affection for each other which most successfully kept the bogey of loneliness away.

All these thoughts buzzed about Ella's head as she thumped her wood block steadily down the length of cloth before her. The kitchen seemed stuffy, the pattern second-rate and the printing patchy. At last, unable to bear it any longer, Ella downed tools, grabbed her coat from the back of the kitchen door, and marched out for air.

It was one of those still, quiet days of winter, when everything seems to be waiting. No breeze disturbed the plumes of smoke from Thrush Green's chimneys. The trees stood bare and motionless. On the hedges small drops of moisture hung; no breath of wind disturbed them, no beam of sunlight lit them to life. The sky was low and of uniform greyness.

'Might as well be in a canvas tent,' thought Ella gloomily, turning her steps towards the lane to Nod and Nidden.

About half a mile along the quiet road she came to a low wall of Cotswold stone, built by a craftsman years before, stone upon stone, so skilfully, that although no mortar had touched it the dry stones had weathered many a gale and blizzard and remained untouched.

Ella leant upon its comforting roughness, took out the battered tobacco tin which accompanied her everywhere, and began to roll herself one of the shaggy vile-smelling cigarettes for which she was noted. Lighting one untidy end she drew in a refreshing breath of strong smoke. Before her, in December haze, stretched mile upon mile of Cotswold country, ploughed fields, grazing pastures, distant smoky woodland, valleys and hills. Here, in this quiet lovely place, Ella knew that she must put her thoughts in order.

Better to face it, she told herself, there was nothing on earth to keep Dimity from marrying if she were asked. What sort of a life did Dim have, when you looked at it squarely? She was bullied and shouted at, did most of the work and got no thanks for it.

'It's a wonder she's stuck it as long as she has,' said Ella aloud to a fat blackbird who had come to see what was going on. With a squawk, her companion fled, and Ella, in her present state of self-chastisement, did not blame him.

And there was no doubt about it that Harold Shoosmith seemed fond of her. He had taken to calling in several times a week and Dimity was unashamedly delighted to see him. He would probably make a very good husband, thought Ella magnanimously. Poor state though matrimony was, it obviously appealed to quite a number of people.

She supposed that they would live at the corner house. Suddenly, Ella found the whole idea peculiarly painful, and tossed her cigarette irritably into a tuft of wet grass. Could it be jealousy, she asked herself? Any man would say so, many women would not. Ella tried to look at the matter soberly again.

Quite honestly, Ella decided, it was not jealousy that made her feelings so acute. She had no desire for marriage herself, though she knew that Dimity's more gentle nature would flower in the married state. Her own mental life was vigorous and creative and afforded her greater satisfaction with every year that passed. Marriage for Ella would be a distraction. She was too selfish not to resent any interruption in her own way of life. For Dimity's happiness she rejoiced. It was just, thought Ella with a wince of pain, that she would miss Dim so much – the shared jokes, the companionship in the little cottage, the modest expeditions and the fun of discussing things with her.

Life was going to be very different with Dim across the green. Could the cottage be endured without her company, Ella wondered? Or would it be best to uproot herself and go elsewhere? It might be fairest to both of them, she decided. Whatever the future held she must let Dimity have her way. She must not be selfish and tyrannical – for too long Dimity had suffered her own over-bearing ways. If this should prove to be Dim's chance of happiness, then, Ella decided, she should take it and she herself would do all in her power to promote it.

Ella took a deep breath of damp Cotswold air, and having cleared her mind, felt a great deal better.

She gave the stone wall a friendly clout with her massive hand, and turned her face towards Thrush Green again.

But still her heart was heavy.

11. Christmas Preparations

THE little town of Lulling was beginning to deck itself in its Christmas finery. In the market square a tall Christmas tree towered, its dark branches threaded with electric lights. At night it twinkled with red, blue, yellow and orange pinpoints of colour and gladdened the hearts of all the children.

The shop windows sported snow scenes, Christmas bells, paper chains and reindeer. The window of the local electricity showroom had a life-size tableau of a family at Christmas dinner, which was much admired. Wax figures, with somewhat yellow and jaundiced complexions, sat smiling glassily at a varnished papier mâché turkey, their forks upraised in happy anticipation. Upon their straw-like hair were perched paper hats of puce and lime green, and paper napkins, ablaze with holly sprigs, were tucked into their collars. The fact that they were flanked closely by a washing machine, a spin dryer and a refrigerator did not appear to disturb them, nor did the clutter of hair dryers, torches, heaters, bedwarmers and toasters, beneath the dining-room table, labelled ACCEPTABLE XMAS GIFTS.

The rival firms of Beecher and Thatcher which faced each other across Lulling's High Street had used countless yards of cotton wool for their snowy scenes. Some held that Beecher's

'Palace of the Ice Queen' outdid Thatcher's tableau from Dickens's *Christmas Carol*, but the more critical and carping among Lulling's inhabitants deemed the Ice Queen's diaphanous garments indecent and 'anyway not Christmassy.' Both firms had elected to have Father Christmas installed complete with a gigantic pile of parcels wrapped in pink or blue tissue paper for their young customers. A great deal of explanation went on about this strange dual personality of Father Christmas, and exasperated mothers told each other privately just what they thought of Beecher and Thatcher for being so pig-headed. The psychological impact upon their young did not appear to have dire consequences. Country children are fairly equable and the pleasure of having two presents far outweighed the shock of meeting Father Christmas twice on the same day – once in the newly-garnished broom cupboard under Thatcher's main staircase, and next in the upstairs corset-fitting room, suitably draped with red curtaining material, at Beecher's establishment.

With only a fortnight to go before Christmas Day Lulling people were beginning to bestir themselves about their shopping. London might start preparing for the festival at the end of October; Lulling refused to be hustled. October and November had jobs of their own in plenty. December, and the latter part at that, was the proper time to think of Christmas, and the idea of buying cards and presents before then was just plain silly.

'Who wants to think of Christmas when there's the autumn digging to do?' said one practically.

'Takes all the gilt off the gingerbread to have Christmas thrown down your throat before December,' agreed another.

But now all the good folk were ready for it, and the shops did a brisk trade. Baskets bulged, and harassed matrons struggled along the crowded main street bearing awkward objects like tricycles and pairs of stilts, flimsily wrapped in flapping paper. Children kept up a shrill piping for the tawdry knick-knacks which caught their eye, and fathers gazed speculatively at train sets and wondered if their two-year-old sons and daughters would be a good excuse to buy one.

At the corner of the market square stood Puddocks', the stationers, and here, one windy afternoon, Ella Bembridge was engaged in choosing Christmas cards.

Normally, Ella designed her own Christmas card. It was usually a wood cut or a lino cut, executed with her habitual vigour and very much appreciated by her friends. But somehow, this year, Ella had not done one. So many things had pressed upon her time. There were far more visits these days, both from the rector and from his friend Harold Shoosmith, and the vague unhappiness which hung over her at the thought of change had affected Ella more than she realised. Today, in Puddocks', reduced to turning over their mounds of insipid cards, Ella felt even more depressed.

But, depressed as she was, she set about her appointed task with energy. She made directly towards the section marked 'Cards 6d., 9d., and 1s.' and began a swift process of elimination. Ballet dancers, ponies, dogs, anyone in a crinoline or a beaver hat, were out. So were contrived scenes of an open Bible before a stained-glass window flanked with a Christmas rose or a candle. It was amazing how little was left after this ruthless pruning. Ella, coming up for air, looked at the throng around her to see how others were faring.

She envied the stout woman at her elbow who picked up all the cards embellished with sparkling stuff and read the verses intently. She had plenty of choice. She admired the way in which a tall thin man selected black and white line drawings of Ely Cathedral, Tower Bridge and Bath Abbey with extreme rapidity. She watched, with bitter respect, a large female who forced her way to the desk and demanded the ten dozen printed Christmas cards ordered on August 22nd, and promised faithfully for early December. Here was efficiency, thought Ella, returning to her rummaging.

At last, she collected a few less obnoxious specimens, paid for them and thrust her way through the mob to the comparative spaciousness of the pavement outside. The clock on the Town Hall pointed to ten past five and Ella decided to try her luck at The Fuchsia Bush, Lulling's most genteel tea-shop.

The Fuchsia Bush's contribution to Christmas consisted of a charming scene arranged on the sideboard just inside the door. Whitewashed branches, from which white and silver bells were suspended, spread above a bevy of white-clad angels. Unfortunately, the whole had been lavishly sprinkled with imitation frost which blew about the shop in clouds every time the door opened. Discriminating customers chose cakes which could easily be shaken free of the glitter and eschewed the iced sticky buns which were normally a fast-selling favourite at The Fuchsia Bush.

At a table near by Ella was delighted to see her old friend Dotty Harmer, her grey hair lightly spangled with blown frost. A cup of tea steamed before her and on a plate lay three digestive biscuits.

'Well, Dotty, expecting anyone?' boomed Ella, dragging back the only unoccupied chair in the tea-shop.

'No, no,' replied Dotty, removing a string bag, a cauliflower and a large paper bag labelled 'LAYMORE' from the seat. 'Bertha Lovelock was here until a minute ago. Do sit down. I'm just going through my list once more. I think I've got everything except whiting for Mrs Curdle. It's usually rock salmon, you know, but I think she's expecting again and whiting must lie less heavily on the stomach, I feel sure.'

'Tea, please,' said Ella to the languid waitress who appeared at her side.

'Set-tea-toasted-tea-cake-jam-or-honey-choice-of-cake-to-follow-two-and-nine,' gabbled the girl, admiring her engagement ring the while.

'No thanks,' said Ella. 'Just tea.'

'Indian or China?'

'Indian,' said Ella. 'And strong.'

The girl departed and Ella unwound the long woollen scarf from her thick neck, undid her coat and sighed with relief.

'Wonder why it's "Indian or China"?' she remarked idly to Dotty. 'Why not "Indian or Chinese"? Or "India or China"? Illogical, isn't it?'

'Indeed yes,' agreed Dotty, breaking a digestive biscuit carefully in half. 'But then people *are* illogical. Look at Father's man trap.'

Ella looked startled. Sometimes Dotty's conversation was more eccentric than usual. This seemed to be one of her bad days.

'What's your Father's man trap got to do with it?' demanded Ella.

'I just want it back,' said Dotty simply. She popped a fragment of biscuit into her mouth and crunched it primly with her front teeth. The back ones had been removed. She had the air of a polite bespectacled rabbit at her repast.

'Oh, come off it!' begged Ella roughly. 'Talk sense!' Dotty looked vaguely upset.

'You know Father gave his valuable man trap to the museum. It was quite a fine working model used in the eighteenth century by Sir Henry – a great-great-grandfather of the present Sir Henry. Father used to demonstrate it to the boys at the grammar school when he was teaching history there.' She paused to sip her tea, and Ella, fuming at the delay, began to wonder if that were all Dotty would say.

Dotty replaced her cup carefully, patted her mouth with a small folded handkerchief, and continued.

'Well,' she said, 'now I could do with it.'

Ella made a violent gesture of annoyance, nearly capsizing the tea tray which the languid girl had now brought.

'What on earth do you want a man trap for?' expostulated Ella. Dotty looked at her in surprise.

'Why, to catch a man!' explained Dotty. Ella made a sound remarkably like 'Tchah!' and began to pour milk violently into her cup.

'I suspect,' continued Dotty, unaware of Ella's heightened blood pressure, 'that someone is stealing my eggs. I could set the man trap at dusk and let the police interview him in the morning.'

'Now, look here, Dotty,' said Ella, in a hectoring tone, 'don't you realise you'd probably break the chap's leg in one of those ghastly contraptions—?'

'Naturally,' replied her friend coolly, 'a man trap works on that principle, and ours was in excellent condition. Father saw to that. He would be quite safe in it till morning. I get up fairly early, as you know, so he wouldn't be in it more than a few hours.' She spoke as though she would be acting with the most humane consideration, and even Ella was nonplussed.

'But man traps are illegal,' she pointed out.

'Fiddlesticks!' said Dotty firmly. 'So are heaps of other traps, but they're used, more's the pity, on poor animals that are doing no wrong. This wretched man knows quite well he is doing wrong in taking my eggs. He deserves the consequences, and I shall point them out to him – from a safe distance, of course – as soon as I've trapped him.'

There was a slight pause.

'You know what?' said Ella interestedly. 'You're absolutely off your rocker, Dot.'

Dotty flushed with annoyance.

'I'm a lot saner than you are, Ella Bembridge,' she said snappily. 'And a lot saner than those chits of girls at the museum who won't let me have Father's property back. I very much doubt if they are legally in the right about refusing my request. After all, Father left all his property to me, and as I say, that man trap is exactly what I need at the moment.'

'You forget it,' advised Ella, rolling a ragged cigarette. 'Pop up to the police station instead and get Sergeant Stansted to keep his eyes skinned. And, what's more,' she added, for she was fond of her crazy friend, 'don't tell him you want the man trap back, or you're the one he'll be keeping his eye on.'

She drew a deep and refreshing inhalation of strong cigarette smoke. This was an occasion, she thought to herself, when a woman could do with a little comfort.

Meanwhile, at Thrush Green, Dimity and Winnie Bailey were busy in the cold and draughty church of St Andrews's.

They were getting the crib ready and had decided that the open-fronted stable, containing the cradle and the figures, really needed re-thatching. They were hard at it, ankle-deep in straw, by the font, as the clock above them chimed half-past three.

Already the church was getting murky. Above their bent heads the tattered remains of regimental flags moved gently in the draughts, and round their cold feet the straw whispered along the tiled floor. The chancel, distant from them, looked ghostly and incredibly old, a place of shadows and mystery.

'I never knew it would be so difficult,' confessed Winnie Bailey, trying to fold refractory straw into a neat bundle. 'We ought to have asked a proper thatcher to do it for us.'

'Never mind,' said Dimity, standing back to survey their handiwork, 'it looks very spruce from a distance. Only this corner to do and then we've finished.'

She gazed ruefully at her small hands.

'I'm full of splinters,' she said. 'When we've finished the roof, let's clear up and have some tea. It's getting too dark to see properly anyway.'

'Lovely!' agreed Winnie with enthusiasm. 'And we'll wash the figures at home.'

In five minutes all was done and the two weary friends were collecting stray wisps of straw when the door opened and the rector came in.

'How goes the work?' he asked. Dimity and Winnie indicated the golden roof with modest pride.

'Experts both,' exclaimed the rector admiringly.

'And very tired ones,' said Winnie. 'We're just going to have tea.'

'Come too,' insisted Dimity, making her way to the windy porch; and the three set off through the winter dusk to Ella and Dimity's home.

After the bleak loftiness of the church the low-ceilinged sitting-room appeared very snug.

The fire glowed with a steady red warmth and the table lamps cast comfortable pools of light on the polished surface of the bookshelves which flanked the hearth. The room was filled with the scent of early Roman hyacinths. A magnificent pale pink azalea caught the rector's eye, and he admired it.

'Isn't it lovely?' agreed Dimity, rolling her gloves together neatly. 'Harold Shoosmith brought it over for us. The fire's just right for toasting and there are some crumpets. Sit down while I fetch the tray.'

The rector seated himself obediently, while the two women

departed to the kitchen, and held out his cold hands to the fire. He seldom saw an open fire these days, he realised with a slight shock. His housekeeper preferred him to use the electric fire as it saved her work, and the good rector was only too willing to fall in with her plans. But, until this moment, he had not realised how much he missed the companionship of a real fire. Here was a living thing that talked with crackling tongues of flame and responded to tending. He really must persuade Mrs Butler to light his fire again. Even if he cleared it up himself in the morning, the rector decided, it would be well worth it.

He leant back into a soft armchair that enfolded him comfortably and looked with pleasure about the little room. How pretty it was, how warm, how welcoming! This was Dimity's work he knew, and how well she did it – timidly, unobtrusively, but with love. His eye lit upon the pink azalea and a small pang shot through the rector's enveloping sense of well-being. Harold Shoosmith, now he came to think of it, also had the knack of making a place comfortable. It wasn't money alone that did it, the rector mused rather sadly, although Shoosmith was a wealthy man compared with himself. It was an ability to choose and place the most suitable objects together, to plan lighting, to attend to small details. The rector thought of his great barn of a rectory, the cold corridors, the lofty Gothic windows and the everlasting cross-draughts from them, and he sighed.

At this moment, Dimity and Winnie returned bearing the tea-things, and the rector seeing a pile of crumpets, took the proffered toasting fork, set about his primitive cooking and felt much more cheerful.

'What news of the statue?' asked Winnie, during the meal.

'Edward's doing very well,' answered the rector. 'He has asked several people to submit designs and we should be able to commission one of them very soon. We've also tried to find Nathaniel's grandson, but we're having some difficulty.'

'What about the daughter?' asked Dimity, pouring tea.

'Nathaniel's daughter? Dead, I fear. She married rather a ne'er-do-well and lived in great poverty somewhere in the West Country. But we hope to trace the son. He should be a man in his thirties now. We all feel that he should be consulted in this business of a memorial to his grandfather. And, as Edward suggested, it would be extremely pleasant if he could unveil it in March.'

'Do you think it will be ready?' asked Winnie doubtfully. Thrush Green was not noted for its punctuality.

'I'm sure of it,' said the rector sturdily. He withdrew a black and smoking crumpet hastily from the fire, blew out the flames and looked at it dubiously. 'Perhaps I'd better keep this one,' he suggested. The ladies agreed with somewhat unnecessary fervour, the rector impaled another crumpet, and tried again.

'I can't think why Ella is so late,' exclaimed Dimity. 'She must have stopped for tea somewhere. I hope she comes back before you go.'

But Ella did not. By the time she had finished her tea at The Fuchsia Bush, said farewell to Dotty whose mind still ran dangerously upon the man trap, and stumped up the steep hill to Thrush Green, Winnie Bailey and the rector had departed.

In the hollow the lights of the little town twinkled in the clear night air, and the rector, walking across to his house looked down upon them with affection. He was much attached to Lulling, and even more to Thrush Green, finding delight in their many aspects. Tonight, snug in its valley, with the dark hills girding it around, the small town appeared particularly endearing.

He gave it a last look before opening his heavy front door and stepping inside.

The house was silent and struck him as cold and damp as he closed the door behind him. He went into his study, switched on the light and looked about him.

The electric fire stood cold and gleaming. Above his desk upon the wall hung a crucifix. The paint was a pale green which gave the room a sub-aqueous look and did nothing to add warmth to the rector's surroundings. The roof was uncomfortably high, and the thin curtains moved restlessly in a continuous draught from the lofty narrow windows.

The rector, remembering the cosiness he had just left, sighed at so much bleakness and switched on the electric fire. It had all been so different when his dear wife had been alive. Life sometimes seemed as forlorn as this study, he reflected.

Then he caught sight of the cross upon the wall, chided himself, and sat down at his desk to work.

12. The Fur and Feather Whist Drive

Miss Fogerty, looking at her restless class of infants, thanked her stars that it was the last afternoon of term. The last day of any term was exhausting, but the one which ended the autumn term, less than a week before Christmas, was enough to try the patience of a saint, particularly if one had the misfortune to be looking after the infants.

Beside themselves with excitement they had fidgeted and squealed, giggled and wept until Miss Fogerty had clapped her hands and said sternly:

'Heads down!'

And when the last head had subsided on to fat young arms folded across the little desks, she had added, for good measure:

'No story until you have been absolutely quiet for five minutes!'

Only then had comparative peace descended upon the classroom, and Miss Fogerty had felt her sanity return.

She walked to the window and looked out at the darkening sky. It was nearly half-past three on the shortest day of the year. Beyond the little playground the fields dropped away to the gentle valley where the path ran to Lulling Woods and where Dotty Harmer's solitary cottage lay. Sheep were grazing on the slope and one sat, chewing the cud, so near the hedge that Miss Fogerty could see it plainly, looking like Wordsworth, with its long nose and benign expression. Blandly surveying the landscape, rotating its jaws in placid motion, it gave Miss Fogerty a blessed feeling of calm.

She turned back to look at the class, much refreshed in spirit. The children lay in varied positions of torpor. Above them hung paper chains in rainbow hues, and here and there a Chinese lantern dangled, swaying gently in the breeze from the windows. Around the room went a procession of scarlet-coated Father Christmases, with white beards made of cotton wool and shiny black paper boots. Normally, all these garnishings would have been taken down before the end of term, but the Thrush Green Entertainments committee had asked for the decorations to be left up as the school would be in use for the Fur and Feather Whist Drive in the evening.

'We will take down everything,' Mr Henstock had assured the two teachers, and the ladies had been truly thankful.

The great wall-clock ticked on past the half-hour and Miss Fogerty returned to the high teacher's chair ready to read the promised story. She looked down upon the bowed heads, ranging in colour from gipsy-black to flaxen, of the class before her. On each desk lay the fruits of the term's industry waiting to be taken home. Spinning tops made of cardboard, calendars, shopping pads, paper mats and Christmas cards jostled together. Soon they would be carried to cottage homes as treasured presents for the families there.

'You may sit up now,' said Miss Fogerty graciously, from her perch.

Thirty-odd flushed faces turned eagerly upward. Three heavy heads remained in sleep upon the wooden desks and Miss Fogerty wisely let them remain there. She opened her little book and raised her voice:

'Once upon a time there was an old pig called Aunt Pettitoes. She had eight of a family; four little girl pigs—'

The children wriggled ecstatically and settled down to hear yet again the tale of the Christmas Pig – Pigling Bland.

Later, that evening, the paper chains swung above the parents and other inhabitants of Thrush Green and Lulling.

The Fur and Feather Whist Drive, whose posters had fluttered bravely from gatepost and tree trunk during the past few weeks, was in progress. The glass partition between Miss Fogerty's and Miss Watson's classrooms had been pushed back with ear-splitting protests from its steel runners. The desks and tables were stacked at one end and upon them lay the prizes. Pride of place went to a large turkey, its snow-white head and scarlet wattles adding a festive touch. Ranged neatly on each side were chickens, pheasants and hares, and everyone agreed that it was a fine show.

The rickety card tables were packed closely together, the tortoise stove was red-hot, and there was a pervading odour of warm bodies and drying country clothes. Faces glistened with the heat, the unaccustomed concentration and the excitement of the chase after the dead game.

At half-time a halt was called for refreshments and the assembly drank coffee or tea from the thick white cups owned and loaned by Thrush Green Sunday School. Conversation was brisk as the brawn sandwiches and sausage rolls were munched, and Nelly Tilling, who dearly loved a whist drive, let her dark eye rove round the company.

Albert Piggott, she decided, was softening up nicely. He had protested against accompanying her to the whist drive, but she had persuaded him 'to look in' towards the end.

'Making me look a fool!' he had muttered audibly. 'What'll people say, seein' you hangin' round me day in and day out?'

'No more'n they're saying now,' retorted Mrs Tilling, with spirit. 'Let their tongues wag. What cause have you to bother?'

He had said no more. He was fast discovering that Nelly Tilling pursued her course very steadily, and it would need a cleverer man than he was to deflect her from it.

She was enjoying her evening. The cards had been in her

favour, and already her score was high. With any luck she should carry home one of the plump birds before her. She appraised them with an experienced eye. The magnificent turkey apart, she decided that she would choose the brace of pheasants to the right of it if she were lucky enough to have the choice.

Meanwhile, with an eye to the future, she heaved her formidable bulk from the chair and made her way to Miss Watson's side.

The headmistress knew Mrs Tilling only slightly, but as she had been sitting alone she imagined that the plump widow had taken pity on her plight, and so was unusually welcoming.

'Terrible hot in here,' began Nelly, throwing off a small fur tippet but lately released from its moth-balls. 'I'd say that stove of yours draws too strong.'

'Indeed, not always,' responded Miss Watson. 'The wind has a lot to do with it. It must have gone round to the north, I think, to pull the stove up like that. Unless the caretaker has put too much on, of course.'

Mrs Tilling permitted herself a perturbed clucking noise.

'Need a lot of knowing, those stoves,' she replied. 'Want several trips a day really to see they're all right!' This was a master stroke as Nelly knew quite well that the present caretaker lived at Nidden and could only attend to the stove once a day. She was delighted to see a pang of anxiety cross Miss Watson's face.

'Can be real dangerous, you know,' she continued smugly, following up her attack. 'I knew a man once as was blown to smithereens by one of them things exploding. He was never the same again.'

'I can imagine it,' said the headmistress.

'And, of course, with children,' Nelly went on forcefully, 'you simply can't be too careful. Especially,' she added, as a happy touch, 'when they're not your own.' She spoke as though the sudden disintegration of one's own offspring could be borne comparatively lightly.

'Oh, I really don't think that would ever happen—' began Miss Watson, a shade doubtfully.

'How often does the caretaker get in?' asked Nelly, with assumed concern. 'I can see by the floors and the paint and that it can't be very often.'

Miss Watson bridled slightly, and Nelly wondered if she had gone too far. Best tackle it slowly, she told herself, if she wanted this job in a month or two.

'Mrs Cooke comes in for an hour or so every evening,' said Miss Watson with a touch of *hauteur*, 'and works very well.'

'Mrs Cooke?' queried Nelly, with wonder. 'Would that be Ada Cooke I was at school with? She used to be in service at Lady Field's place. Always worked well, I heard. Leastways she did before she had that row of children. Must tie her – can't do what you used to with a gaggle of kids under your feet, of course.'

Privately, Miss Watson wholeheartedly agreed with Mrs Tilling about Ada Cooke's decline in reliability, but wild horses would not have dragged agreement from her. She looked about her, hoping to catch sight of someone to whom she could retreat.

Nelly Tilling's dark eyes saw all and she shot her last arrow before her quarry escaped.

'It's a lovely job for her here, I must say. I fairly envy her and that's flat. Plenty of scrubbing and polishing is just what I can tackle to, as anyone'll tell you. I'd be proud to help you out, Miss Watson, should Ada ever be took bad.'

Miss Watson smiled graciously, murmured her thanks and fled to the other side of the room. Nelly, watching her agitation, was well content.

'Will you return to your tables, please?' shouted the rector, who was acting as Master of Ceremonies, above the clatter of cups.

The second half was about to begin.

The trouble started an hour later when the whist drive was over. The snow-white turkey had gone to a stranger who lived quite four miles away, Nelly Tilling, rejoicing, had collected the coveted pheasants and the rest of the prizes had been distributed, when the rector gave his customary little speech of thanks to all who had helped.

'You will all want to know how much this evening has brought in,' he added. 'I'm delighted to say that five pounds ten shillings and ninepence will be added to the Nathaniel Patten Memorial Fund.'

There were polite exclamations and a little clapping, but above this pleasant noise rose a belligerent voice. It belonged to Robert Potter, a pork butcher in Lulling, renowned not only for the excellence of his chipolata sausages but also for his fiery temper.

He was a formidable sight as he shoved back his chair with one huge red hand and faced the rector, his red face flaming above the bull neck.

'I'd like to know why the money's going to this Nathaniel Patten fund and not to the Children's Home as it always has done. Us folks in Lulling had no say in the matter.'

He thrust his face forward and shouted even more loudly.

'And what's more, I speak for plenty of others who don't hold with their money being grabbed by a lot of Thrush Green lay-abouts to spend. Nathaniel Patten's as much Lulling's property as Thrush Green's. We'd a right to be consulted at our end of the town.'

The rector surveyed his critic soberly. Inwardly he was

shaken by this attack. Outwardly, he appeared unruffled. Not even the few cries of agreement which arose, somewhat sheepishly, from various quarters of the packed room, seemed to perturb him. When he spoke it was with quiet authority.

'I'm sorry to hear that there is this feeling about. The posters stated quite plainly that the proceeds would be devoted to the Memorial Fund. I can't help feeling that it would have been better to have spoken earlier about this disagreement.'

The rector's reasonable tone went a little way to calming Robert Potter's choler, but he still spoke truculently, and obviously relished the support of those who had voiced their resentment.

'Well, there it is! I don't hold with the money going to the Fund. Nathaniel Patten may have been a good man – I'm not saying he wasn't – but as a strong chapel-man I don't like to see a statue raised to a churchgoer when it's my money involved. Straight speaking never done no harm, they say, and that's what I'm doing now.'

There were cries of 'Hear, hear' and 'Good old Robert!' from a few men desirous of showing-off before the women.

The rector suddenly found himself wishing that Harold Shoosmith were there. In the midst of his mental turmoil he was surprised to find how much he was coming to rely on the good sense of this new friend. But he was used to facing trouble alone and braced himself in the thick of parochial battle.

'I will report your objection to our committee, Mr Potter,' he answered courteously. 'Meanwhile, I suggest that we say our farewells in the spirit of goodwill which should be present at this time.'

He smiled cheerfully at his flock as they collected coats and hats, scarves and gloves and made for the door. There they were, the good meek sheep, the silly ones, and the one or two black ones. His eye caught sight of Robert Potter's thick red neck and he wished that he had a shepherd's crook in his hand to catch away that infectious member of his flock from the rest.

'I will have a word with you after the next committee meeting,' said the rector politely.

'Hmph!' grunted Robert Potter, and departed stiffly.

The next morning Mr Henstock looked in at the school again. A band of helpers was busy taking down the paper chains and the Chinese lanterns, and the village school was beginning to look more like itself again. In a day or two's time Mrs Cook from Nidden would set about her scrubbing, her younger children left in charge of those of riper years.

The rector helped for a short while and then wandered into the playground. The blue smoke from a winter bonfire blew across from Harold Shoosmith's garden next door, and there, in the distance, he could see his friend vigorously forking garden rubbish on to the blaze.

Without more ado the rector made his way there and told Thrush Green's latest resident what had occurred the night before. Despite his light tone Harold Shoosmith noticed that the rector seemed worried. His response was heartening.

'Forget it until after Christmas. Ten to one it will all blow over. We can mention it at the next meeting in the New Year, but if my guess is correct there will be no more heard of Mr Potter's objection.'

He bent down to collect a wet armful of dead leaves and branches, tossed them upon the bonfire, and sniffed happily.

'Smells wonderful, doesn't it?' he said to the rector. 'I've been looking forward to a great smoky winter bonfire for thirty years.'

'And I've been looking forward to a winter holiday somewhere abroad for about the same length of time,' confessed the rector. 'I suppose the truth of the matter is that we're none of us ever completely satisfied.'

A woman's voice, calling shrilly from the house, caused them to turn their heads.

'That means coffee,' said Harold Shoosmith, giving a last loving poke to the fire with his fork. 'Betty will have one ready for you too, I'm sure.'

'It will be very welcome,' said the rector politely, following his host to the back door.

13. Christmas Eve

DUSK fell at tea-time on Christmas Eve at Thrush Green. There was an air of expectancy everywhere. The windows of St Andrew's church glowed with muted reds and blues against the black bulk of the ancient stones, for inside devoted ladies were putting last minute touches to the altar flowers and the holly wreath around the font.

Paul Young and his friend Christopher lay on their stomachs before the crackling log fire in the Youngs' drawing-room. They were engaged in fitting together a jigsaw puzzle, a task which Paul's mother had vainly hoped might prove a sedative in the midst of mounting excitement. They were alone in the room and their conversation ran along the boastful lines usual to little boys of their age.

'I never did believe in Father Christmas,' asserted Christopher, grabbing a fistful of jigsaw pieces which Paul had zealously collected.

'Here!' protested Paul, outraged. 'They're all my straight-edged bits!'

'Who's doing this?' demanded Christopher belligerently. 'I'm a visitor, aren't I? You should give me first pick.'

There was a slight tussle. Christopher twisted Paul's arm in a business-like way until he broke free. Panting, Paul returned to the subject of Father Christmas.

'I bet you did believe in him! I just bet you did! I bet you *went on* believing in Father Christmas until I told you. So there! Why, I knew when I was four!'

'So what? I bet you still hang up your stocking!' bellowed Christopher triumphantly. Paul's crimson face told him that he had scored a hit.

'So do you,' retorted the younger boy, not attempting to deny the charge. They fell again into a delicious bear-hug, rolling and scuffling upon the hearthrug, and finally wrecking the beginnings of the jigsaw puzzle which had been so painstakingly fitted together.

The sound of carol singing made them both sit up. Dishevelled, breathless, tingling with exercise and the anticipation of Christmas joys, they rushed into the hall.

The carol singers were a respectable crowd of adult inhabitants of Thrush Green, all known to the boys. So far this year the only carol singers had been one or two small children, piping like winter robins at the doors of the larger houses on Thrush Green for a few brief minutes, and then dissolving into giggles while the boldest of them hammered on the knocker.

The boys watched entranced as the carol singers formed a tidy crescent round the doorstep. Some held torches, and the tall boy who had written on the blackboard at the meeting to decide about the memorial, supported a hurricane lamp at the end of a stout hazel pole. It swung gently as he moved and was far more decorative in the winter darkness, as it

glowed with a soft amber light, than the more efficient torches of his neighbours.

Joan Young opened the front door hospitably, the better to hear the singing, and the choir master tapped his tuning fork against the edge of the door, hummed the note resonantly to his attentive choir, and off they went robustly into the first few bars of 'It came upon the midnight clear.'

Their breath rolled from their tuneful mouths in great silver clouds, wreathing about their heads and the sheets of music clenched in their gloved hands. In the distance the bells of Lulling Church could be faintly heard, as the singers paused for breath.

The smell of damp earth floated into the hall, and a dead leaf scurried about the doorstep adding its whispers to the joyful full-throated chorus above it. The bare winter trees in the garden lifted their arms to the stars above, straining, it seemed to young Paul, to reach as high as St Andrew's steeple.

The boys gazed enraptured, differences forgotten, strangely moved by this manifestation of praise. It seemed to be shared by everything that had life.

A mile away, Doctor Lovell's wife Ruth roamed their small sitting-room restlessly. Her husband was tinkering with the car in the nearby garage, and she wondered whether she should call him or not.

She felt extraordinarily shaky and rather light-headed. The baby was not due for another week, but babies do not wait upon their coming, as Ruth as a doctor's wife well knew. She leant upon the mantelshelf and ran her mind over the preparations she had made.

Everything awaited the baby upstairs. One of the Lulling doctors, an old friend called Tony Harding, was to attend her, and her daily help had promised to live in for a fortnight when the birth took place. Her sister Joan would be with her much of the time and keep an eye on the house-keeping.

Luckily, she remembered, she had stuffed the turkey and had prepared a delectable trifle. The cupboard was crammed with food, the beds had been changed, the laundry awaited collection, the flowers were fresh and the house had been garnished especially well for the Christmas festival.

Ruth heaved a sigh of relief. She could afford to forget her household cares and think of this momentous happening after so many weeks of weary waiting.

A particularly vicious spasm gripped her, and when it passed the girl made her way to the window and opened it. The cool night air lifted the fair hair from her hot forehead. The faint sound of Christmas bells floated from afar on the refreshing breeze.

'John!' called Ruth, 'I think you'd better fetch Tony Harding.'

A small black car, rather shabby and sagging a little at the springs, was drawn up outside Albert Piggott's cottage. It had travelled a long way throughout the short winter day.

Inside the house, Ben Curdle and his wife Molly, sat at table with Mr Piggott eating fried bacon and eggs cooked by Molly. Upstairs, in the room which had been her bedroom, her small son slept in a drawer pulled out from the chest, and stowed neatly on the floor at the foot of his parents' bed.

Molly's eyes took in the shining stove, the clean walls, the scrubbed brick floor and the scoured sink. It was quite apparent to her that a woman had been at work, and one who knew her job well. Her father had been grudgingly welcoming an hour ago, but had made no mention of anyone helping him in the house. She looked across the tablecloth at him, munching as morosely as ever.

'Place looks nice, dad,' she said.

'Ah! I does what I can,' said Albert, never raising his eyes from his plate.

'What about your cooking?' enquired his daughter.

'I gets by,' said Albert flatly. Molly caught her husband's twinkling eye upon her, and winked mischievously.

'I've brought a chicken ready for the oven,' said Molly, 'so you'll have a good meal tomorrow. How's the stove drawing these days? D'you ever sweep the flues?'

'Now and again,' answered Albert, polishing his plate slowly with a piece of bread guided by a grubby forefinger. 'I got me own work, you know. That church don't get no smaller.'

Ben shifted his long legs and spoke.

'I went over to have a look at Gran's grave when we arrived. Looks a bit neglected. Don't no one ever see to it?'

Albert Piggott grunted.

'Can't get it all done by myself,' he muttered.

'I'll tidy it up tomorrow,' said Ben steadily. 'That's not right to see the old lady under half a peck of hay. Not seemly, to my way of thinking. Who's responsible for the graves then?'

'Those as want regular clipping, and the plants on 'em tended proper, pays me a bit extra,' said Albert. He put the piece of bread in his mouth and chewed it noisily. Ben watched him levelly.

'I'll see you're paid,' he said quietly.

Molly seemed about to speak, but a rapping on the door checked her. As they looked up, startled by the noise, the door opened and Nelly Tilling's face, rosy and arch, peered round it.

'Oh my law! You 'ere again?' said Albert Piggott, with a groan.

Construing this ejaculation as a welcome, the stout widow came into the room, closed the door behind her, and dumped a laden basket on the table.

'There!' she panted breathlessly. 'Your Christmas dinner, Albert dear!'

Molly drew in a sharp breath. So this was the answer to her secret questioning! This was the mysterious scourer and scrubber, the cook and companion! And just how far had this gone, Molly asked herself with unreasoning fury? Before she could speak, Ben put a large brown hand over hers and pressed it warningly. Molly held her tongue, and waited, as quietly as Ben, to see how her father would respond.

A dusky flush had crept over his unlovely features and his jaw dropped. To say that Nelly Tilling had taken the wind out of his sails was to put it lightly. He was staggered at her effrontery. He had made quite sure that she knew she would not be wanted while his daughter stayed in the house, and this was open defiance. But what could a chap do, he asked himself, when a woman set her cap at him so boldly and brought a square meal with her into the bargain? He took refuge in truculence.

'We ain't that short of food, Mrs Tilling,' he answered gruffly. 'Don't know what brought you on this errand, I'm sure.'

Nelly Tilling's dark eyes flashed dangerously.

'Ho ho!' she said, bridling. 'Very hoity-toity, some of us, aren't we? And since when 'ave I been Mrs Tilling to you, Albert Piggott? It's been Nelly all right these last few weeks while I've been cleaning up this pigsty for you.'

She hoisted the basket to her arm again belligerently.

'Seeing as I've had this flung back in my face I may as well leave you for good,' she continued. 'Leave you to your swilling and swearing and the filthy ways you was used to before I put you straight!' She paused to get her breath, her ample bosom rising and falling violently beneath her tightly-buttoned coat.

Suddenly Molly felt sorry for her. It must have taken her hours to prepare all the good things that she could glimpse under the snowy cloth which covered the basket. And she had trudged all the way from Lulling Woods carrying that weight, thought Molly, for what thanks! She found that all her old disgust at her father's mean ways was returning fast. First his behaviour in the matter of old Mrs Curdle's grave, and now this betrayal of Nelly Tilling's kindness, inflamed Molly's sense of fitness. She rose from the table and took the infuriated widow's arm.

'You come and sit down, Mrs Tilling,' she said gently. 'I think it was real nice of you to think of Dad at Christmas-time. We're just making a pot of tea, so have some with us.'

Somewhat mollified, Nelly sat down on a chair by the door, her basket by her feet. Albert, dumbfounded by this unexpected alliance against himself, decided to retreat.

'Want somethin' a bit stronger, lad?' he asked Ben, hoping in this way to assert his independence before Nelly and Molly, before taking flight.

'If you like,' said Ben politely.

'Come on next door then,' said Albert, rising hastily from the table.

He was past Nelly and through the door in half a minute. Nelly looked grimly down her nose, her massive arms folded upon her chest.

Ben paused by her chair and touched a large shoulder gently. He smiled at her, his eyes crinkling in the way which had so charmed his wife. Nelly looked less grim.

'I'll look after him for you,' said Ben gently, and was rewarded with Nelly's grateful smile.

There was silence for a short time in the little room, broken only by the singing of the kettle on the shining hob. Then Molly said shyly:

'Thank you for looking after my dad. He's not much of a hand at housework and all that.'

Nelly permitted herself a gusty sigh.

'That he ain't,' she said honestly. 'Don't go thinking too much of this, Molly. I've only been acting neighbourly, and it fair cut me to the quick to see him so short with me just now. More than 'uman flesh and blood can stand, it was.'

'He's a bit awkward,' confessed Molly, in sublime understatement. 'The place looks beautiful. I could see someone who knew what she was doing had been at it.'

Nelly gave a gratified smirk and accepted her tea graciously. She loosened her coat and prepared to enjoy this tête-à-tête. After ten minutes' polite conversation she rose to go, and Molly decided that now was the time to show Nelly that she was her friend.

'Would you like to see my baby?' she asked.

'I'd love to,' said the widow, following Molly up the narrow stairs so recently brushed down by her own sturdy hand.

The baby lay deep in slumber, his eyes screwed tightly shut and his small mottled fists clenched each side of his mop of black hair. Nelly clucked maternally.

'Eh, what a little love!' she wheezed rapturously, after the steep ascent. 'Don't he favour his dad? You're a lucky girl, I must say.'

She rummaged in her handbag, drew out half a crown and slipped it gently beneath the sleeping child's small fingers.

'Oh no!' protested Molly.

'Ah yes,' said Nelly firmly. 'It'll bring me good luck to cross your baby's hand with silver. And, believe me, I can do with it!'

She made her way on tiptoe to the door and descended the narrow stairs, followed by Molly.

'I'll leave the basket,' she said, as she stood in the doorway outlined against the darkness of Thrush Green. 'Use what you want, and I hope you'll all have a very happy Christmas.'

'But won't you come and join us for dinner?' asked Molly, now genuinely fond of Nelly after her appreciation of the baby.

'No, dear,' said Nellie firmly. 'It's real nice of you, but Christmas is a family time.'

She turned and made her way into the darkness.

'I'll be seeing Albert afterwards,' she said, and in her tone was something which brooked no good for that backslider.

It seemed to Molly, as she closed the door, that her father had met his match in more ways than one.

Ella and Dimity were spending the evening by the fire. Both women were tired with the bustle of the day. Dimity had made one trip to Lulling in the morning, only to find, on her return, that she had forgotten several urgent articles needed during the Christmas holiday, which meant another journey down the steep hill and up again, during the afternoon.

She was touched by Ella's offer to make the second trip, but had refused, for dear Ella had been very busy delivering Christmas presents of her own making to nearby friends.

Now they sat comfortably enjoying the peace after the storm. Ella smoked one of her rank shaggy cigarettes, her sturdy brogues propped up on a string stool, while Dimity knitted placidly a matinée coat for Ruth Lovell's coming baby. Upstairs, carefully packed in one of Thatcher's dress boxes was a thick ribbed cardigan for Ella's Christmas present, only finished just in time, for Dimity had been obliged to work at it only in Ella's absence from the room, as she intended it to be a surprise.

Ella, too, had packed a garment in one of Thatcher's boxes for Dimity's Christmas present, but it was not of her own making. She had bought a soft fluffy blue dressing-gown for her friend on one of her trips to London. Too long, she decided, had Dimity wrapped her thin form in a shabby grey flannel garment which she admitted to buying long before the war. Since Ella's heart-searching, by the Cotswold stone wall on her lonely walk, she had done her best to be less selfish, and it had not gone unnoticed.

'I thought we'd have eggs for supper,' said Dimity, letting the knitting fall into her lap. 'Boiled or scrambled, Ella dear?'

'Boiled,' replied Ella. 'Less bother. No filthy saucepan to clean up either.'

Dimity began to wind the wool round the needles, but Ella got up before her.

'You stay there, Dim. You look a bit done up. I can do boiled eggs easily enough.'

'Oh, Ella, you're much too kind! You're tired yourself!'

'But I'm not going to early service tomorrow, don't forget.'

'I feel I must,' said Dimity, clasping her thin hands earnestly. 'The rector does so like to have a full church at early service. Harold's going I know.'

Ella stubbed out her cigarette violently. She seemed embarrassed at the mention of their new friend's name, thought Dimity, somewhat bewildered.

'He's a good chap,' said Ella gruffly, and stumped towards the kitchen.

Left alone, listening to the crashing of saucepans from the kitchen, Dimity pondered on Ella's generous heart. She had been even more thoughtful lately, she told herself – more gentle, more sympathetic. She remembered Ella's unusual embarrassment when she had spoken of Harold Shoosmith. They said that love often had a mellowing influence, and certainly Ella had always thought highly of the newcomer. Could Ella's recent gentleness have anything to do with affection for their handsome friend, asked Dimity in wonderment?

Darkness thickened over Lulling and Thrush Green. The Christmas tree twinkled and blazed in the market square dwarfing the stars above to insignificance.

Excited children for once went willingly to bed, stockings clutched in their rapacious hands and heads whirling with delirious thoughts of joys to come. Exhausted shop assistants sat at home soaking their aching feet in warm water. The patients in Lulling Cottage Hospital thought of the long gruelling day ahead, complete with boisterous surgeons carving turkeys, paper hats, hearty nurses singing carols and all the other overwhelming paraphernalia of Christmas in the wards, and they shuddered or smiled according to temperament. Housewives, flopping wearily in armchairs, congratulated themselves upon remembering the decorations for the trifle, the cherry sticks for the drinks and other last minute details until they were brought up short by the horrid thought that in the pressure of so much unaccustomed shopping they had completely forgotten salt and tea, and now it was too late anyway.

But away from the lights and worries of the town the quiet hills lay beneath a velvety sky. No wind rustled the trees and no bird disturbed the night's tranquillity. Sheep still roamed the slopes as they had that memorable night so long ago in Palestine, and low on the horizon a great star, bright as a jewel, still held out an eternal promise to mankind.

14. Christmas Day

'It might almost be September instead of Christmas Day,' exclaimed Dimity, as they walked down their garden path on the way to the Baileys' house. 'Look, Ella, there are still some marigolds out!'

It was certainly mild, and the midday sun had a slight warmth. Ella snuffed up the fresh air like an old war-horse and nodded her shaggy locks with approval.

'Something to be thankful for, anyway,' she responded. 'I can't say I relish these Dickensian Christmases with snow up to your knees and a lot of wild skating parties. Far more likely to make a full churchyard, they are, thea a nice seasonable green Christmas – whatever old Piggott may say!'

Winnie Bailey was at her door to meet them.

'Happy Christmas,' she said. 'You're the first to arrive. It's just an *elderly* party. And a very small one.'

It was a punctual one too, for Ella and Dimity had only just greeted the doctor when Dotty Harmer, the rector and Harold Shoosmith arrived together. The doctor dispensed drinks and the chatter began.

'Doctor Lovell rang up a few minutes ago,' confided Winnie to Ella quietly! 'The baby is due to arrive today.'

'Bad luck,' said Ella. Winnie Bailey's eyebrows rose.

'Only because it will have its birthday on Christmas Day,' explained Ella hastily. 'Always tough on children, I think. Who's with her?'

'Joan, and the daily, and young Lovell's mopping and mowing about, I gather. Mrs Burridge, the aunt who stayed here during the war, was going to come, but decided she couldn't. Do you remember her?'

'Do I not!' said Ella explosively. 'I'm not a womanly woman, as well you know, but the way that cat used to leap to her feet when Dim and I came into the room, and then guide us solicitously to the nearest chair as though we were senile, used to make my blood boil. She must have been a good ten years older than we were anyway!' Ella's normally rosy face had turned quite purple with wrath at the memory.

'Even Donald admitted that she was the embodiment of malice,' agreed Winnie calmly. She became conscious of the rector's mild eye turning upon her, as he overheard this remark, and went over to speak to him. Dimity and Harold were at the window watching the world of Thrush Green taking the air in readiness for Christmas dinner. They appeared happily engrossed and Ella, turning from the sight abruptly, found Dotty Harmer at her elbow. She seemed agitated.

'I don't want to be too long,' she whispered to Ella. 'I've left a pumpkin pie in the oven. It's an American dish – I had an American cookery book given to me some time ago and I thought I'd like to try something rather different for Christmas Day.'

'If it's anything like marrow,' said Ella firmly, 'you're welcome.'

'It's a great delicacy,' insisted Dotty. 'The Americans have it on Thanksgiving Day, I gather. Though why they should want to give thanks for losing touch with their mother country, I never could imagine,' added Dotty, with a touch of *hauteur*. 'My father always referred to what the Americans call "The War of Independence" as "The American Rebellion." The new headmaster was quite unpleasant about it, and he and Father had words, I remember.'

'Ah well,' replied Ella, in a conciliatory tone, 'it all happened a long time ago, and the Americans seem to be struggling along quite nicely without us. Can't expect your children to cluster round your knee for ever, you know.'

Dotty did not appear completely persuaded by this philosophy, but allowed Doctor Bailey to take her glass to be refilled, and then fluttered after him to change her mind. Ella remained alone on the sofa and all her old unhappiness suddenly flooded over her.

To all appearances this annual sherry party was like all the others. There was the blue and white bowl filled with Roman hyacinths and sprigs of red-berried holly. There was Winnie, as pink and white and gay as ever, wearing the deep blue suit that she had worn last year. And, she supposed, she herself presented the same tough leathery aspect that she always did.

But what a change had occurred in the last year! What a cataclysm had gone on in her heart! Nothing was the same, nothing was stable. Life had been turned topsy-turvy, and turmoil and conjecture tossed her to and fro. She looked again at the serene room, her old friends, and the placid indifferent countenance of Thrush Green through the window, and Ella could have howled like a dog with abject misery at the hopelessness of ever trying to explain how different all her loved and little world was to her this Christmas Day.

At half-past one, in Albert Piggott's cottage, Molly was washing up the débris of the Christmas feast. Her father and Ben were accustomed to taking their main meal of the day at twelve o'clock for they were early risers, and Molly too had risen soon after six after feeding her baby.

Ben wiped up vigorously, and his father-in-law leant in the doorway considerably impeding the progress. Occasionally Ben thrust a piece of crockery into his unwilling hands for him to put away in the cupboard. Conversation was carried on above the clatter at the sink and the cries of young George above who was impatiently awaiting his two o'clock feed. The child had been named after Ben's father, the favourite child of old Mrs Curdle, who had lost his life in the war. Doctor Bailey, to whom Molly had proudly shown her son that morning, maintained that he was the image of that baby he had delivered almost fifty years before.

'We'll leave you in peace this afternoon,' said Molly. 'Ted and Bessie Allen want to see the baby and we'll be there till they open the pub at six.'

'No need to hurry back on my account,' answered Albert sourly, squinting at a glass mug, in an unlovely way, to see if Ben had polished it sufficiently.

'Must be back by then,' said Molly firmly, 'to put George to bed. But if you want to go out – to see Nelly Tilling, say – don't wait about for us.'

It was pure mischief that had prompted Molly to speak of the widow, and Albert rose swiftly to the bait.

'Don't go getting ideas in your head about Nelly Tilling,' he growled. 'She be a rare one for chasing the men, as I've no doubt you knows well enough. She ain't 'ad no encouragement from me, that I can say.'

'More fool you,' said Ben cheerfully. 'You'd be lucky to get her. Look after you well, she would.'

'Too dam' well,' grunted Albert. 'Never let a chap forget 'e signed the pledge before his mother's milk 'ad dried on 'is lips.' He sniffed noisily. 'I 'opes I've got more sense than to put me 'ead in that noose!'

'Well, it seems to be expected,' said Molly lightly. 'Miss Watson asked me about her when I took the baby past her house this morning.'

'Miss Watson? That old faggot?' shouted Albert, shaken to his marrow. 'What call 'as she got to go linking Nelly Tilling and me?' He breathed heavily for a minute.

'She ain't never been right since she got hit on the head a month or two back,' he continued. 'Must've left her a bit dotty.'

'First I've heard of it,' said Ben. 'What happened?'

Albert gave a garbled account of the robbery at the schoolhouse in the autumn.

'And the police,' he said, banging his hand on the dresser for emphasis, 'is fair scuppered. As a matter o' fact, I'm on the look-out for the chap meself.'

'Well, I hope you find him,' said Molly, undoing her apron. 'Poor old soul! Fancy hurting an old lady like Miss Watson! Why, she must be over fifty!'

Albert looked at himself in the kitchen mirror, and smirked.

'That ain't so old,' he said, with unusual jauntiness, brushing his damp mouth with the back of his hand. He caught the eye of his son-in-law and gave a watery wink.

Miss Watson, happily ignorant of the furore she had caused, was sitting snugly in the schoolhouse parlour, spending her Christmas afternoon in writing letters of thanks.

She was engaged in giving a long account of the morning's service at St Andrew's to Miss Fogerty whose Christmas holiday was being spent with an octogenarian aunt at Tunbridge Wells.

'The church,' wrote Miss Watson in her precise copperplate, 'looked lovely, decorated with holly, red and white carnations and Christmas roses on the altar. You would have enjoyed the singing, and the rector's sermon was very fine, on the theme of generosity. Very much to the point, I thought, in a community like Thrush Green, where back-biting does occur, as we know only too well. It made me feel that I really must try and *forgive*, even if I cannot *forget*, that wretched man who attacked me.'

Miss Watson put down her pen for a moment and gazed thoughtfully out upon Thrush Green. The room was tranquil, and she was enjoying her holiday solitude. Now that she had time to collect her thoughts Miss Watson had gone carefully over and over the incidents of that terrifying night, but further clues escaped her. From the first she had felt that her attacker was someone that she knew. In the weeks that followed she scrutinised the men of Lulling and Thrush Green to no avail. But she had not, and would not, give up hope. One day, she felt certain, she would recognise the brute and he would be brought to justice.

The winter sun was beginning to turn to a red ball, low on the horizon. Above it, long grey clouds, like feathered arrows, strained across the clear ice-blue sky. Somewhere a blackbird sang, as though it were a spring day, and Miss Watson, suddenly finding the room stuffy, opened her window the better to hear it.

A family passed near by, crossing the green, no doubt bent upon taking tea with relatives. That indefinable Christmas afternoon atmosphere, compounded of cigar smoke, best clothes and new possessions crept upon Miss Watson's senses, as she watched the father bending down to guide the erratic course of his young son's new red tricycle. Screaming with annoyance, the child beat backwards at his father's restraining hand. The mother's protests, shrill and tired, floated across the grass to the open window.

'There are times,' said Miss Watson smugly to the cat, 'when an old maid has the best of it.' And she turned, with a happy sigh, to her interrupted letterwriting.

While Miss Watson finished her letter and her neighbours slept or walked off the effects of their Christmas feasting, Ruth Lovell looked, for the first time, upon her daughter.

She weighed seven pounds and two ounces, had a tiny bright pink face mottled like brawn, and from each tightly-shut eye there protruded four short light eyelashes. But to Ruth, to whom good looks meant a great deal, the most alarming thing was the shape of her daughter's head, which rose to a completely bald pointed dome.

'Will she always look like this?' asked Ruth weakly of Tony Harding, who was busy packing his bag neatly. She did not like to seem ungrateful for his ministrations, but she was beginning to wonder, in the daze that surrounded her, whether he had not helped her give birth to a monster.

'Heavens, no!' was the brisk reply. 'That head will have gone down in a day or two. Believe me, you're going to have a very pretty little girl.'

Ruth smiled with relief and settled the baby more comfortably in her arms.

'It was too bad of me to bring you out on Christmas Day,' she said apologetically. 'I'm terribly sorry.'

'Think nothing of it,' replied the doctor, straightening up. 'All in the day's work.'

He made for the door.

'There's a very good precedent, you know,' he said cheerfully, and vanished.

The red sun had dropped behind the folds of the Cotswolds, and the short winter day was done by the time Albert Piggott shuffled across to St Andrew's to ring the bell for evensong.

Two or three bicycles were already propped against the railings, and a figure moved hastily away from them as Albert approached.

'Who's that?' asked Albert, switching on a failing torch. By its pallid light he recognised Sam Curdle.

'Bike fell over. Just proppin' it up,' volunteered Sam, a shade too glibly. Albert looked at him with dislike and suspicion. He wouldn't mind betting Sam had been looking in the baskets and the saddlebags for any pickings, but as far as he could see the fellow held nothing in his hands. Albert grunted disbelievingly.

'Got yer cousin staying at my place,' he said at last. Sam did not appear delighted.

'Don't mean nothing to me,' he said spitefully. 'Ben and me never had no time for each other. He can go to the devil for all I care.'

'Well, that's your business,' said Albert, shuffling on again. 'I'll say good night to you.'

'Good night,' replied Sam shortly, and set off in the direction of Nidden. Albert, pausing on the church path, looked after his disappearing figure. A growing conviction shook his bent frame with excitement.

'If that fellow didn't do poor old Miss Watson,' thought Albert to himself, 'I'll eat my hat!'

And taking that greasy object from his bald head, he entered the church and made his way towards the belfry and his duty, highly elated.

PART THREE

The New Year

15. A Bitter Journey

On New Year's Day the rector and Harold Shoosmith set out on a long journey.

Four letters and a telegram, with a prepaid answer, had all failed to elicit any reply from Nathaniel Patten's grandson. His address had been found with the help of many people, and it appeared that William Mulloy lived in a remote hamlet in Pembrokeshire.

'The only thing to do,' Harold said, 'is to call on the fellow and try to get some answer from him. We'll stay the night somewhere. It's a longish drive and we may as well do it comfortably.'

After a few demurrings on the part of the conscientious rector, who had various meetings to rearrange in order to leave his parish for two days, the two men had decided that the first day of the New Year, which fell on a Friday, would suit them both admirably.

It had turned much colder. An easterly wind whipped the last few leaves from the hedges, and dried the puddles which had lain so long about Thrush Green. People went about their outdoor affairs with their coat collars turned up and their heads muffled in warm scarves. Gardeners found that digging in the cruel wind touched up forgotten rheumatism, and children began to complain of ear-ache. In Lulling the chemist displayed a choice selection of cough mixtures and throat lozenges. Winter, it seemed, was beginning in earnest.

The two men breakfasted very early, Harold Shoosmith in his warm kitchen on eggs and bacon, and the rector walking about his bleak house with a piece of bread and marmalade in his hand, as he did his simple packing. It had seemed selfish to expect his housekeeper to rise so early, and she had not suggested it. She wished him a pleasant journey before retiring for the night and said she would take the opportunity of washing the chair covers in his absence. With this small crumb of comfort the rector had to be content.

He felt rising excitement as he crossed Thrush Green from his gaunt vicarage to the corner house. The Reverend Charles Henstock had few pleasures, and an outing to Wales, albeit in January and in the teeth of a fierce easterly wind, was something to relish. It was still fairly dark, only a slight lightening of the sky in the east giving a hint of the coming dawn. One or two of the houses around the green showed a lighted window as early risers stumbled sleepily about their establishments.

The dignified old Daimler waited in the road outside Harold's gate. Its owner was busy wrapping chains in a piece of dingy blanket, and stowing them in the boot.

'Just in case we meet icy roads,' said Harold, in answer to the rector's query, and Charles Henstock marvelled at such wise foresight.

The car was warm and comfortable. After talking for the first few miles the two settled down into companionable silence, and the rector found himself nodding into a doze. He was happy and relaxed, pleased to be with such a good friend, and relieved to leave Thrush Green and its cares behind him for two days. He slumbered peacefully as the car rolled steadily westward.

Harold Shoosmith was glad to see him at rest. Nothing had come of the protest at the Fur and Feather Whist Drive, and it had been generally decided to press on with the arrangements for the memorial. But the rector had worried about it considerably, Harold Shoosmith knew. To his mind, the rector had a pretty thin time of it, and if he himself had ever been saddled with the sort of housekeeper Charles endured he would have sent her packing in double-quick time, he told himself. There were some men who were born to be married, and who were but half-men without the comfort of married estate. The good rector, he realised, was one of them, and he fell to speculating about a possible match for his unconscious friend. It would seem, as he reviewed the charms of the unattached ladies of distant Thrush Green, that the rector's chances were slight, thought Harold unchivalrously.

He braked suddenly to avoid a swerving cyclist and his companion woke with a start.

'Good heavens! I must have dropped off,' exclaimed the rector, passing a hand over his chubby face as if to brush away the veils of illicit sleep. 'Where are we?'

'Just running into Evesham,' replied Harold. 'You finish your kip.'

'No, no indeed,' protested the rector, yawning widely. 'I'm not in the least tired.'

He straightened himself and watched the neat bare orchards roll by. The sky above was an ominous dark grey and a wicked wind caught the side of the car now and again, making it shudder off its course. By the time they reached Hereford heavy rain, pitilessly cold, swept the streets, and here they stopped for lunch.

'A real beast of a day,' commented Harold, as they waited for their mutton chops. Through the window of the hotel they watched the rain spinning like silver coins on the black shiny road. 'But as long as it rains it won't snow,' he continued. 'I've a feeling we'll see plenty of that later on this winter.'

'I'm no weather prophet,' confessed Charles Henstock, 'but

Piggott says we're in for several weeks of it. I hope he's wrong.'

'Piggott's a gloomy ass,' said Harold. 'Never so happy as when he's miserable, as they say. I shouldn't take his prognostications too seriously.'

'He's often right about the weather though,' said the rector, rubbing his cold hands. He held them to the meagre warmth of the one-bar electric fire with which the hotel hospitably welcomed its visitors to a lofty dark dining-room of tomb-like chill. Three paper roses in a tall glass vase, one pink, one red and one yellow, decorated each table, standing squarely in the middle of the frosty white tablecloth.

'Make the most of the place, don't they?' commented Harold ironically, surveying the scene.

'It looks very clean,' ventured the rector charitably, and indeed, used as he was to bleak surroundings, his present circumstances seemed comparatively cosy.

Luckily, the soup was hot and the mutton chops succulent, and the two friends continued on their journey much refreshed. Soon they were among the dark Welsh mountains, whose majesty was veiled in curtains of rain.

'We shouldn't have much trouble in finding a room tonight,' said Harold, driving through a water splash that covered the windscreen momentarily. 'There won't be many people out in this lot.'

'I hope Piggott will keep the stoves well stoked,' said the rector, his thoughts turning again to Thrush Green. 'It's choir practice tonight, and there are so many colds about.'

'What's a cold here and there?' asked Harold robustly, stopping at a level crossing.

'I always think my poor wife died of a neglected cold,' mused the rector, as though to himself.

'I'm sorry,' said Harold, chiding himself. There was silence in the car. In the distance a faint whistle told of the approach of the train. 'You must miss her very much,' went on Harold, trying to make amends.

The rattling of the train across their path prevented any response. The great gates were swung back by a fat little Welshman with a wet coat draped over his head and shoulders and the car moved over the rails to continue its journey.

'I miss her more than I can say,' said the rector at last. He looked sadly at the road before him, but his friend had the impression that he was glad to talk of this matter which he had kept to himself for so long. He made a sympathetic noise, but no verbal comment.

'It's a strange thing,' continued the rector, 'that one doesn't remember how the dead looked during the last months of their life. When I think of Helen it is always as a young woman.'

His voice grew more animated.

'She was so gay. She sang, you know, about the house. And she made it so cheerful with flowers and fires. We had a little cat too, but Mrs Butler doesn't like animals, and when it died I thought it best not to get a kitten.' His voice died away, and they drove for almost a mile before he spoke again.

'Somehow the house too seems dead now,' he added, almost apologetically.

'If you don't mind my saying so,' said Harold, 'you'd be better off without that housekeeper of yours.'

'Mrs Butler?' asked the rector, astonished. 'I really think she does her best for me. Why, she's even taking the opportunity of washing the chair covers in my absence.'

'That's as may be,' said Harold stubbornly. 'She does a bit, I dare say, but she could do a lot more. You never have a decent fire, for one thing, and it's my belief she skimps on the cooking.'

Such plain speaking rendered the rector temporarily dumb. But on turning over the words in his mind, he admitted to himself that there was a great deal of truth in them.

'But what can I do?' asked the rector pathetically. 'If I complain, she'll go, and it really is an appalling job to get anyone else suitable. I shudder when I think of some of the applicants I interviewed. There was the young woman with pink hair—' He stopped, arrested by the memory.

'Don't I know,' sympathised Harold. 'I've had it too, don't forget. Enough to make me think of marrying, it was at times,' he said lightly. 'And I'm not a marrying man, I fear.'

The words were said so cheerfully and in such a matter-of-fact tone that their full impact did not dawn on the rector for some minutes. But later he was surprised at the warm glow of delight that suffused him. Could it be possible that his friend had no matrimonial designs upon any one of the ladies of Thrush Green whose hearts he had so pleasurably fluttered since his advent?

'Some are the marrying sort, and some not,' continued Harold, looking at three small children fighting in a village street. 'Frankly, I would say that you are.'

'I think you may be right,' agreed the rector, in a small voice. 'But I've very little to offer a woman.'

'Don't come that modest-martyr stuff over me,' implored Harold. 'You think about it. That's my advice. And think about sacking Mrs Butler too, or at least tell her to pull her socks up.'

'I really don't think I'm equal to it,' confessed the rector. But whether he was referring to his hopes of matrimony, or the dismissal of his housekeeper, no one could say.

They stayed the night in a small Pembrokeshire town within a few miles of their quarry.

'How did you sleep?' asked the rector, at breakfast the next morning.

'Apart from some Welsh-speaking plumbing that was woven around the room, I heard nothing at all,' said Harold. 'I feel ready for the hunt. One thing, the rain's stopped.'

It was true, but the sky still had a steely greyness about it, which boded no good, and the wind still blew evilly from the east. The dining-room, however, was a little more comfortable than the one in which they had lunched, and two electric bars warmed a smaller room, there was a modest carpet and a real fern on an intricately carved stand in the window. Two moth-eaten heads of deer graced the wall above the marble mantelpiece, and the rector, who abhorred blood sports, averted his gaze from the glassy eyes above him.

By ten o'clock they were approaching the little hamlet where they hoped to find William Mulloy. The rector looked forward to the meeting with interest, but Harold Shoosmith felt considerable excitement at the thought of coming face to face with the grandson of the man he had esteemed for so long. Would there be any facial resemblance, he wondered, as the Daimler threaded its way in a gingerly manner down a narrow rough lane? He had been looking out ancient photographs and the copy of a portrait of Nathaniel for the proposed sculptor's benefit, and he had become very fond of the plump Pickwickian countenance of the good old missionary.

'We should be there,' observed the rector, looking about him. 'We've taken the left-hand fork and gone about a quarter of a mile. Now, where is the pair of cottages?'

They stopped the car, studying the rough sketch map that the waiter at the hotel had given them. The bare fields stretched away on each side, and from the tussocky bank near by a thrush whistled, surveying them with a bright inquisitive eye.

A small girl with a very dirty face appeared suddenly in the lane. She was carrying an empty milk bottle.

'Could you tell us where Mr William Mulloy lives?' asked Harold politely.

'Behind the trees,' answered the child, in a sweet sing-song, nodding to a clump near by. Now that their attention was directed there, the two men saw a wisp of smoke rising from a hidden chimney.

'Thank you very much,' said Harold, preparing to get out of the car. The child smiled and continued her journey towards the larger road, still clutching the milk bottle.

'I suppose the milkman leaves milk at the top of the lane,' said the rector, genuinely interested in these domestic arrangements. 'This lane must peter out eventually. What a deserted sort of place.'

They collected the few papers about the proposed memorial from the back of the car and made their way on foot to the cottage. It was one of a pair, both ramshackle in appearance, with every window tightly closed. Harold knocked at the front door with some difficulty, for the knocker was rusty and was stiffly encrusted with ancient paint.

There was a sound of footsteps, then a bolt was drawn back, and a struggle began within to tug the door from its fast-clinging frame. At last a breathless voice called to them:

'Step round to the back, will you? The door's stuck.'

Obediently the two men traversed a narrow concrete path which skirted the house so closely that Harold had difficulty in remaining upon it.

At the back door waited a small pale woman with hollow cheeks. She wore an overall and a pair of fawn carpet slippers.

'Are you from the insurance?' she asked. She spoke with a strong Welsh accent and looked alarmed.

'Indeed, no,' said Harold reassuringly.

'We're looking for Mr Mulloy,' said the rector gently. 'Are you, by any chance, Mrs Mulloy?'

'Well yes,' said the woman doubtfully. 'In a manner of speaking, I am.'

'That's splendid,' said Harold heartily. 'We wondered if your husband could spare us a few minutes.'

'He's not here,' said the woman, and for a moment it looked as though she were about to shut the door.

'Now please—' began Harold in an authoritative voice, but the rector motioned him to keep silence, and spoke instead. His experienced eye had noticed the sudden pain which had caused the woman to draw in her breath sharply.

'We won't bother you for more than a moment,' he assured her gently, putting a plump hand on her thin arm. She looked at him and gave a small smile. The rector noticed that she had very few teeth, which accounted for the hollow pinched look of her sad face.

'We wrote to your husband several times,' he continued, 'but I fear the letters must have gone astray.'

'No, they're all here,' said the woman unexpectedly. 'You'd better come in out of the wind.'

As they followed her through a small kitchen to the living-room at the front of the house, the rector became conscious of someone following him. The small girl, now holding a full milk bottle, was entering too.

'My little girl,' said the woman. 'Put the milk in the cupboard, Dulcie.'

'Dulcie!' exclaimed Harold. 'Named after her grandmother perhaps? That was Nathaniel's daughter's name.'

'That's right,' said the woman, without much enthusiasm. She closed the door between the kitchen and living-room and motioned the men to sit.

'We'd better explain,' began the rector, and gave a brief account of Thrush Green's plans.

'So you see,' broke in Harold, 'we would like to see how your husband feels about it. Does he work on a Saturday morning? We had hoped to find him at home.'

The woman answered dully.

'He don't call this home any more. The truth is, he's left me.'

'Left you?' echoed the rector, with compassion in his voice.

'Left you?' echoed Harold, with dismay in his. What if the wretched fellow had left the country altogether? A fine wasted journey they would have had, thought Harold Shoosmith with disgust.

Mrs Mulloy took four letters and an unopened telegram from the mantelpiece and handed them to Charles Henstock.

'I kept them thinking he might be back. The first came the day after he went. But he's never come.'

'I'm so very sorry,' said the rector. 'We had no idea of this, naturally.'

'Do you know his address?' asked Harold practically. Mrs Mulloy's face took on a mutinous look, and the rector spoke hastily.

'You see, we've come such a very long way, and I have to be back tonight ready for my Sunday services tomorrow. It would be so kind of you if you would tell us where he is. We might be able to see him if he is not too far away.'

The woman's face softened as she looked at the rector's cherubic countenance. The man need have no fear, thought Harold watching her, of not having any charm over women. It's partly that child-like look and partly his genuinely kind heart, he decided, content to leave the negotiations in his friend's competent hands.

'He's left me for a low common woman I wouldn't demean myself to speak to,' burst out Mrs Mulloy. 'He's at her house now, no doubt. Two miles up the valley, and the name is Taylor. It's a farmhouse. Anyone will tell you.'

She stopped suddenly, and the rector saw that her eyes were wet.

'Does he provide for you?' he asked.

'Not a penny,' she said bitterly. She was talking to the rector as though no one else were present, and Harold sat very quietly. 'I'm to go to court next week.'

'How do you manage?' said the rector.

'I've got a job at the big house. Dulcie comes there after school for her tea, then we come home. I don't go Saturdays, unless I'm wanted specially.'

'I see,' said the rector. He put the letters in his pocket, and held out his hand. 'We won't worry you any further, Mrs Mulloy,' he said. 'But I think we will try to see your husband, while we're here. I will write to you, if I may, when I return, and perhaps I can be of some help. I hope so.'

The woman held his hand trustingly and gave him a watery

smile. Harold rose to make his farewells and they made their way through the kitchen to the bleak garden. Dulcie was cutting up cabbage in a business-like way with an enormous fierce-looking knife. The scene quite terrified the rector.

'Here,' said Harold firmly, at the door, 'buy something for the little girl from me.'

'Thank you, sir,' said the woman, almost sketching a bob, as she took the note. 'And I hope you both have a good journey back.'

'How brave of you to give her money outright like that,' said the rector, when they were back in the car. 'I just couldn't do it!'

'You did the real dirty work,' answered his friend. 'She'd have told me nothing. Now let's go and find the malefactor.'

The farmhouse, by Cotswold standards, was a humble affair. It consisted of a two-storey box, which had once been white-washed, with a grey slated roof. A jumble of outhouses, made of corrugated-iron and rough timber, clustered at its side, and the sound of animals could be heard coming from them. They drove the car up a steep track, axle-deep in mud, as near to the house as was possible, before picking their way on foot to the front door. A black and white sheepdog, tied to a post with a stout rope, barked hysterically at them, standing on its back legs and pawing the air in its frenzy.

Before they had time to knock, the door was opened by a young woman with a cigarette in her mouth.

'Yes?' she asked shortly, squinting at them through the smoke that curled into her eye. 'You from the insurance?'

Harold Shoosmith began to wonder if all strangers in Pembrokeshire were welcomed in this way. What was it, he wondered, about their appearance which suggested that they were connected with an insurance company? Or why, for that matter, were the householders of Pembrokeshire so anxiously awaiting the arrival of insurance men? It seemed a pity that he would never know the answer.

'We've called to see Mr Mulloy,' began the rector diffidently.

'He's here. Come in,' said the woman without preamble, and they followed her into a small smoky room almost filled with a gigantic three-piece suite upholstered in shabby black leather. It reminded Harold Shoosmith of the railway station waiting-rooms of his boyhood as he looked at the buttons dimpling the back of the couch.

From the depths of one of the chairs a massive man arose. His shirt collar was open and he wore no tie. His creased grey flannel trousers were tied round his vast stomach with a dressing-gown cord. His hair was long, his eyes bleary, his teeth were stained brown with tobacco smoke and Harold Shoosmith judged that his last shave took place three, or possibly four, days before. If this were Nathaniel's grandson then he was glad that the spruce old man could not see his descendant.

'Mr Mulloy?' he asked abruptly, disappointment sharpening his tone.

'That's right,' said the man. 'My wife send you?'

'She told us the way,' replied Harold. 'But we came to see you, not your wife.'

'Take a seat,' said the woman, removing a pile of newspapers from one end of the couch and tossing them pell-mell into the corner of the room. A startled mew gave evidence of a cat's presence in the murky corner, but it remained in hiding. 'I'll clear out if you're going to talk business.'

'Really, there's no need,' protested the rector. 'It's just a little matter of a memorial.'

'Who to? The wife?' asked the man, guffawing loudly. 'I'd give you a bit towards that, wouldn't I, Ethel?'

The woman smiled grimly, but made no comment. The rector looked disconcerted, and not a little shocked.

It was Harold who took command at this interview, and in a few curt phrases outlined the purpose of their errand. William Mulloy slouched forward as he listened, his stomach heavily pendulous inside his grubby shirt, sucking his revolting teeth and swallowing noisily. The gentle rector, almost overcome by the rank smells of the stuffy room, prayed that their visit would be brief.

'What d'you want me to do about it?' asked William Mulloy, when Harold finished. 'Want money, do you, to put up this 'ere statue? You'll get not a farthing from me, I can tell you. I heard enough about that old bundle of misery from my mother – she was just such another Holy Joe – and I want nothing to do with it.'

Harold Shoosmith's face so openly expressed the disgust he felt that the rector decided that he had better intervene.

'We had no intention of asking you to contribute towards your grandfather's memorial. We simply wished to find out if you were interested. We felt that it was common courtesy to get your opinion on our venture.'

'Well, my opinion, gents,' said William Mulloy, with a shrug of his massive shoulders, 'is that the lot of you are plain barmy. But if you like to throw good money away by sticking up some tin-pot effigy to that dismal old sky-pilot, why, you're welcome. But don't expect me to take any interest in it. My life was made a misery with his ideas. If it hadn't been for my dad giving me a good time now and again I reckon I'd have gone loopy the way my mother kept talk, talk, talk about what grandad would have said.'

'He was a very fine man,' said Harold, with controlled passion. 'A man who did so much good in his life that he is remembered with affection and respect all over the world.'

'Aw! Stow it,' yawned William Mulloy. 'You and my ma would have made a good pair.' He heaved his great bulk from the chair and held out a sticky fat hand.

'I'll say good-bye. Sorry you've had a long journey for nothing. But you've got my blessing for this crack-brained scheme, if that's what you came for. If there's any money over, you might think of the old chap's descendants, you know.'

Harold Shoosmith could not bring himself to take the extended hand, and contented himself with nodding and hastening to the door; but the rector shook it politely and murmured his farewells to them both.

The sheepdog kept up its insane barking as they backed away from the house and regained the lane. Harold seemed speechless with fury and disappointment, and the rector spoke with some diffidence.

'He obviously takes after the ne'er-do-weel father,' he commented. 'Not a very attractive person, I thought.'

'What I thought,' remarked Harold grimly, 'is unprintable.' He pulled the wheel round savagely and set off on the long journey home.

They stopped only once, and that was at Ross, for a late lunch. By that time their disappointment and shock had somewhat evaporated. The rain had ceased and the wind had dropped, so that they were able to enjoy the winter beauty of the wooded countryside.

The air was iron-cold and hurt the lungs. The sky's menacing greyness was tinged with the slight coppery colour which precedes a snow-storm, and the two men were glad to regain the warmth of the car after the walk from the hotel.

Darkness fell earlier than usual and they drove for several

hours through the ominously still blackness. As they climbed the last steep hill to the haven of Thrush Green the first few snowflakes began to waver across the windscreen.

'Hello,' said Harold, 'here it comes at last.'

They got out of the car stiffly and stretched themselves luxuriously. Around them the snow whispered its way to the ground, although as yet, it failed to cover it.

'It's been a wonderful break,' said the rector, by way of thanks. 'Though disappointing perhaps.'

'At least we know where we are,' replied Harold. 'We certainly don't need Mr Mulloy's help in the unveiling ceremony. Come inside and get warm.'

The rector held his face up to the whirling snowflakes as Harold fumbled for the key. It was good to be back again at Thrush Green. He remembered, with sudden pleasure, the conversation on the way down and realised, with deep happiness, that more had been resolved, for him, than simply the unveiling of Nathaniel Patten's memorial.

16. Snow at Thrush Green

THE inhabitants of Thrush Green woke on Sunday morning to find an eerie lightness reflected from their ceilings and a hushed white world outside their windows.

Snow was still falling, steadily and gently, and had settled by breakfast time to a depth of two or three inches. The steep Cotswold roofs, white beneath their canopies, showed sharp and angular against the leaden sky which promised more snow. A light powdering had settled along the branches of the chestnut trees, and round the many bird-tables of Thrush

Green the footsteps of dozens of small birds made hieroglyphics as they came seeking charity.

The reactions of the Thrush Green folk to their changed world varied considerably. Paul Young, waking to see the whiteness on his ceiling, leapt from his bed with wild delight and rushed to the window. Heaving it up, he scraped the new snow from the sill and crammed it rapturously into his mouth. The crunch with which it clove deliciously to the roof of his mouth, before melting into icy nothingness, entranced him. In the distance he could see the milkman, trudging to each house from his van and leaving a neat row of footprints to each door. The sight of Thrush Green stretching smooth and virginal, in all its wide spaciousness, offered a challenge to run and jump, to roll and frolic, and to make that vast anonymity his own, signed with his own ecstatic markings. Shaking with excitement, he thrust himself into his clothes.

Albert Piggott's response was typical as he gazed morosely from his bedroom window.

'Would 'appen on a Sunday. All that muck trod into the coconut matting in the aisle when the folks come to morning service! This'll take some clearing up!'

Gloomily, he stumped down the narrow stairs to prepare his breakfast.

Nelly Tilling, in her distant cottage near Lulling Woods, took one look at the snow, another at the threatening sky, and went barefoot and in her vast nightgown to check her provisions. There was flour in plenty in the enamel bin. Sugar, butter, tea and rice gave her silent comfort from one shelf, and bottled fruit and jam of her own preparing from another. Onions dangled from the beam above her head, jostled by a bunch of dried herbs. A shoulder of mutton waited to be cooked and there were eggs and cheese in plenty. She could live comfortably for a week at least, she decided.

But firing was a different matter. There was some coal, but that was lodged in a small shed at the end of the garden, together with logs which needed splitting for kindling wood. Nelly, suddenly conscious of the chilly floors, returned to the bedroom to dress. She must collect as much fuel as she could manage to store indoors before the snow engulfed the little shed.

Dotty Harmer, in her solitary cottage in the hollow behind Thrush Green, was also up betimes. Her spirits had soared as she surveyed the dazzling purity of the fields which surrounded her. Snow had always delighted her. She remembered the tobogganing parties which she and her small friends had enjoyed on the sledge made for her one Christmas by her schoolmaster father. How well he had fashioned it and of what stout stuff was proved by the fact that it still hung in Dotty's lean-to at the side of her house. Two or three winters before she had dragged home her shopping on it from Lulling in just such weather, she recalled, and had later lent it to her neighbour to draw fodder to some cattle at the end of the small valley.

Unlike Nelly Tilling she did not think of her own provisions, but her first anxiety was for her chickens at the end of the garden, and for Mrs Curdle and the new kittens. She put on a man's overcoat and a pair of wellington boots and made her way through the scrunching snow, with a double measure of corn in the zinc dipper.

The chickens were delighted at this largesse and pecked at the yellow grains which studded the unaccustomed whiteness of the run. Dotty threw a large groundsheet over the wire roof, so that the snow should not get too thick. She thrust a bundle of straw into the hen house for extra warmth, and cut three large winter cabbages from the patch. These she shook free of snow and dropped into the run. She could do no more, she decided, filling the water bowl. They were well provided for.

As she bent to her tasks, she was conscious of an ache across her chest as she breathed. For the past week she had been troubled by a cold and a cough which kept her awake at night.

'It's this cold air,' said Dotty to the hens, who were almost delirious with joy at so much food at one time. 'I'd better take some of my coltsfoot and raspberry cordial. Good-bye, my dears.'

Dotty turned and battled her way through the whirling snowflakes to the shelter of the cottage. She was not to see her dear hens again for many a long day.

'D'you know what?' demanded Ella, bursting into Dimity's bedroom. 'The whole place is full of dam' snow!'

'Indoors, do you mean?' asked Dimity, wrenched thus brutally from sleep and understandably bewildered.

'No, no, no!' said Ella testily. 'Just everywhere.' She stumped across to Dimity's window, a thickset figure wrapped in her old red dressing-gown, and gazed with dislike at the wintry scene.

'All in the trees,' went on Ella disgustedly, as though this really was the last straw. 'All over the roofs,' she added despairingly.

'It's usual, you know, with snow,' responded Dimity, with unwonted irony. 'How deep is it?' She sat up in bed to get a glimpse of the whirling flakes.

'About a couple of inches, I should say,' answered Ella. 'But plenty more to come. Let's have breakfast in our dressing-gowns, Dim, and then get dressed and clear the paths.'

The thought of action against this infiltrating enemy cheered Ella at once, and the two drank their coffee and ate their habitual toast and marmalade in the snug kitchen and made plans like a pair of generals at the beginning of a campaign.

'We must bring the spades inside tonight,' said Ella briskly, 'in case we have to dig ourselves out tomorrow. It looks quite likely. I'll bring in extra coke, coal and wood, and it might be a good idea for you to take extra milk today. The milkman's on the other side of the green. Let's put a note out now.'

'You think of everything,' said Dimity, with admiration. 'I must put out more food for the birds, poor things, before I go to church.'

'I suppose you have to?' queried Ella. 'It'll be perishing cold, and everyone will be teeming with revolting germs. There's flu about, they tell me.'

'Yes, of course I must go,' said Dimity with quiet firmness. 'Charles would be most upset, if I failed to go.'

Ella's massive hand held the coffee pot arrested in mid-air as she looked at her friend.

'I believe you're right,' she said slowly.

It snowed for two days without ceasing, and an easterly wind, which sprang up during Sunday night, caused drifts several feet deep. Banks of snow reached to the windows of 'The Two Pheasants' and completely covered the white fence at the village school hard by. The lane to Nod and Nidden was impassable by Tuesday, and the two hamlets were cut off from the outside world. The snow ploughs were out along the main road from Lulling to the north, but the steep hill was so slippery that little could be done there. The older inhabitants spoke longingly of the handrail which had once lined the path to the town, as they slithered, with socks over their wellingtons, to gain a foothold on the slope.

The Lulling shops were under-staffed, for many of their assistants lived in outlying villages and were unable to get into the town. Delivery vans were few and far between, and neighbours lent each other cupfuls of sugar and packets of tea as supplies became short.

Influenza had spread in the little town, with such alarming rapidity that the preparatory school attended by Paul and his friend Christopher had closed for a week in the hope that this might arrest the spread of infection.

After the first few days of joy Paul soon became bored. Snow showers continued intermittently throughout the week, and the nights were bitterly cold. His mother only allowed him to play outside for short spells, but towards the end of the week she invited Christopher to play during the hours of daylight, as both boys were in the rudest health and were obviously not going to succumb to the prevailing plague.

Paul was delighted to have company. In the afternoon, a watery sun tried to shine through scudding clouds, and Joan said that they might go out for a time.

'Let's go to the camp,' said Paul as soon as they were outside. 'It's years since we were there.'

They crept through the hole in Harold Shoosmith's hedge, skirted the shrubbery which had protected the path from the worst of the snow and struggled along to the tree.

Here a deep drift made it impossible for them to go further. The snow had been swept into a vast billow delicately patterned with a tracery of whorls and curves. Beyond it stretched the snowy valley, with Dotty's cottage a mere hump in the vastness. The house looked dead. No smoke rose from the chimney, no one moved behind the closed windows and there was no sign of life anywhere.

Paul, used to seeing Dotty pottering about her colourful garden, hearing the squawking of her hens and the companionable mewing of Mrs Curdle as she followed her mistress about, suddenly felt a spasm of inexplicable fear.

'There's nobody there,' he said, gripping Christopher's arm. 'It looks all wrong.'

'Only because of the snow,' said Christopher sturdily. 'It's all this whiteness. Makes you feel sick after a bit, my mother says, because our eyes are used to lots of colours.'

This scientific explanation did not satisfy Paul.

'I don't mean that,' he protested. 'It looks as though Miss Harmer's gone away. But she *never* goes away, Chris. Never! She's got the animals to look after.'

While Paul gazed with anxiety at the house and his friend gazed at him with perplexity, a terrifying thing happened. One of the upstairs windows slowly opened, and a witch-like form, with grey eldritch locks hanging round a paper-white face, sagged over the sill. A skinny arm began to swing an old-fashioned hand-bell, and the eerie notes clanged across the snowy wastes to the frightened boys.

'It can't be Miss Harmer,' whispered Paul, white as a ghost.

'It is!' said Christopher shakily. 'And she's ill or something. She wants help.'

'We can't get through that drift,' answered Paul, with a hint of relief in his voice. 'Let's shout to her and tell her we'll get help.'

They cupped their hands round their mouths and began to call to the small wild figure. The bell kept up its erratic din, now loud, now soft, but the toller gave no sign of hearing the answering cries from the boys.

At that moment, Harold Shoosmith, clad in fishing waders and an oilskin, appeared from his garden and approached the children.

'How long has this been going on?' he asked.

They spoke together in a rush, too relieved to see help to worry about their trespassing.

'It's Miss Harmer—' began Paul.

'She must be ill,' said Christopher. 'She's just come to the window.'

'We were shouting to tell her we'd get help,' continued Paul. 'It's too deep for us to get through.'

'I'll go and get a spade,' said Harold. 'You wait here,' he added, 'I may need you.'

They watched him plough back towards the house. The figure still sagged from the window, the bell hanging silent in one hand.

'Mr Shoosmith's coming!' shouted Paul encouragingly. He felt brave with relief, and almost began to enjoy the adventure.

'We're going to help him!' bellowed Christopher, not to be outdone.

By way of reply it seemed, the bell gave a convulsive ring and fell from the inert hand into the muffling snow below. The figure slid out of sight, presumably to the bedroom floor. Alarm seized the boys again.

'It's the shock,' said Paul aghast. 'We've jolly well killed her!'

For once, Christopher was too stunned to reply. At this moment Harold appeared again, armed with two spades and a coal shovel.

'She's fallen down,' quavered Paul.

'Then there's no time to lose,' said Harold briskly. 'We'll see how we get on, but if it's deeper than we think, one of you must run for more help.'

He set to, and cleared a way through the first deep drift, the boys flinging the snow energetically aside, pink-faced with excitement and exercise. Luckily, they soon came to shallower snow, and Harold proceeded alone, the snow almost to the top of his waders, until the garden gate was reached.

'Stay where you are,' Harold ordered. He struggled over the gate. He was beginning to wonder just what he would find inside the house. No sound had come from it, and he was secretly most alarmed.

He had to dig his way again through the garden. The snow had drifted into grotesque shapes against the hen house and the cottage.

After ten minutes' struggle he reached the back door. He was perspiring with his exertions, and the oilskins were horribly stuffy. He found the door unlocked, and entered the kitchen.

It was very cold and quiet. An unpleasant smell, compounded of stale food, drying herbs and cats, greeted him. The clock had stopped, the barred grate was full of grey ash, and a spider had spun its web from a cold saucepan on the hob to the wall near by.

'Anyone at home?' called Harold. 'Are you there, Miss Harmer?'

There was no reply. Harold stamped the snow from his boots and mounted the stairs. The sound of frantic mewing reached his ears from behind a closed door. He undid the latch and out bolted Mrs Curdle, followed unsteadily by four young kittens. They vanished downstairs, presumably in search of food.

The only other bedroom had its door propped open. There Dotty lay, crumpled on the floor, by the open window.

Harold was relieved to find that her eyes were open and that she was attempting to speak. She looked desperately ill, and her breathing was loud and stertorous. He lifted her on to the untidy bed and covered her gently.

'Just lie there for a moment,' he said. 'Now don't worry about a thing.'

He strode to the window and leant out.

'Cut back home, Paul,' he shouted, 'and ask your mother to ring Doctor Lovell. I'm going to carry Miss Harmer to my house. She's not well.'

'Me too?' asked Christopher.

'No. I may need you,' said Harold. 'Hang on there.'

Dotty was becoming agitated, rolling her untidy grey head from side to side restlessly. Harold went closer to hear what she was trying to say.

'Poor cats! Poor chickens! No food!' croaked Dotty.

'What about you?' asked Harold. 'When did you eat last?'

She shook her head.

'I'm going downstairs to get you a hot drink, and I'll see to the animals,' he promised. 'Then we must get you out of this.'

He closed the window, switched on an archaic electric fire, which looked none too safe for his peace of mind, but was better than nothing, and departed downstairs.

The cats mewed plaintively, and he explored the tiny larder. A bottle of milk was now solid cream cheese, but a dozen or more tins of cat food, prudently purchased by Dotty at the onset of the blizzard, cheered him. He opened two, scooped out the contents and let the cats wolf it down. Dotty's provender was harder to find, but he discovered some Bovril and an electric kettle and soon returned to the bedroom with a steaming cup.

The warmth of the bed and the room seemed to have given poor Dotty more strength. She sipped her Bovril gratefully. Harold wondered how she would react to his suggestion that he carried her bodily up the hill to his own house. It was quite apparent that she was desperately ill. Ideally, she should not be moved, but the house was cold, without food, and inaccessible. If he could get her to Thrush Green then Lovell could take over. She was as light as a bird, and the path had been made. It should not be too difficult a journey, but he must wrap her up well. He looked at the shabby coats hanging behind the door with a speculative eye.

'I'm taking you to Thrush Green,' he said, with gentle

authority. 'Then Doctor Lovell can have a look at you. You'll have to let me carry you, you know.'

'No need,' wheezed Dotty, surprisingly acquiescent. 'Sledge downstairs.'

'How splendid!' cried Harold. 'I'll go and get it ready.'

He found old Mr Harmer's masterpiece, and some leather straps, hanging in the lean-to. He collected some spare blankets from the room in which Mrs Curdle and her kittens had been incarcerated and made a warm comfortable bed upon the sledge, and then returned for his patient. It seemed most practical and decorous to wrap the old lady in the warm bed clothes which already surrounded her, and carrying the unwieldy bundle, Harold stepped carefully down the staircase and deposited her on the sledge. He returned for a pillow, and leant from the window to shout to his assistant who was busy making a snow man.

'Be ready,' he called. 'I'm bringing Miss Harmer on a sledge. Are you warm enough?'

'Boiling!' said Christopher, scarlet in the face.

Harold closed the window, switched off the fire, gathered up the pillow and returned downstairs.

'Drink,' said Dotty, looking exhausted.

Harold hurried to get a glass of water.

'Cats!' said Dotty, with weak exasperation. Harold meekly filled a bowl and put it on the floor.

'I promise you,' he said solemnly, 'that someone will come and look after all the animals, as soon as we've got you safely in bed again.' He strapped the small figure safely on to the sledge, tucked an old mackintosh over and under the whole contraption and set off through the snow to Thrush Green.

The journey was comparatively easy, and Dotty stood the jolting well. Harold was glad, however, of Christopher's

help, and tireder than he cared to admit when he finally arrived, by way of the garden, at the corner house's back door.

To his relief, Joan Young was there with Paul awaiting him, and he left her to put Dotty to bed in the spare room while they waited for the doctor.

Whisky and soda in hand, he stood at the sitting-room window watching the trees dropping flurries of snow as the wind caught them. If there were much more of this weather, thought Harold gloomily, they would not get Nathaniel's statue erected in time. He resolved to find out more from Edward Young about the progress he had made.

At that moment, young Doctor Lovell appeared and Harold took him upstairs to the patient.

Paul and Christopher were on the landing, gazing from the window. It occurred to Harold that the two boys might well be tired and hungry too.

'Come down to the kitchen,' he said, 'and we'll find some biscuits and a hot drink.'

'Not *hot*,' begged Paul.

'What then?' asked Harold. 'Iced lemonade?' he added amusedly, looking at the bitter world outside.

'Oh please!' breathed the two fervently, following him downstairs. Shuddering, he led them to the refrigerator.

'Hospital job,' said Doctor Lovell, crashing downstairs. 'Can I use your phone?'

'Carry on,' said Harold and waited until all was arranged before making more enquiries.

'Bronchitis, perhaps pneumonia,' said the doctor. 'Basically, of course, it's malnutrition. I shouldn't think she's eaten a square meal for years. But she'll be all right. Keeps fretting about her pets.'

'Tell her I'll go down myself while she's away,' said Harold. 'It's no great distance.'

'You're what's known as a good Samaritan,' said the doctor, making for the door. 'And one who was just in time, I may say. She wouldn't have lasted much longer without attention – and then where would all the pets have been?'

The arrival of the ambulance broke short their conversation. Curtains twitched at several windows on Thrush Green, and one or two bolder spirits emerged from their cottages the better to see who might be the victim. The arrival of Doctor Lovell had not gone unnoticed. The sight of the ambulance increased the excitement. What could have happened to Harold Shoosmith?'

It was with considerable mystification that the watchers saw Harold himself striding beside the stretcher a few minutes later. Who could he have been harbouring in his house all these years? Must be a deep one – that newcomer.

After the tedium of several house-bound days it was delightful to speculate about the drama unfolding before their eyes. Here was mystery, here was excitement, here was food for endless gossip! Thrush Green was agog.

Harold Shoosmith was a good Samaritan in more ways than one.

17. Two Clues

SNOW shrouded Thrush Green for over a week and throughout that time Harold trudged daily to Dotty's cottage to care for the animals. People were heartily sick of the snow. Travelling was difficult, supplies were getting scarce, influenza spread alarmingly and tempers were sorely frayed.

It was with the utmost relief that the good folk of Lulling and Thrush Green saw their barometers rising and the weather-vanes veering towards the south-west. Soon a warm wind enveloped the Cotswolds and within two days little rivulets ran down the hill to Lulling, the snow slithered with a heartening rushing sound from the steep tiled roofs, and the green grass could be seen again.

People emerged from their houses as joyfully as children let out from school. It was wonderful to smell the earth and grass again, and more wonderful still to feel a gentle warmth blowing instead of the withering east wind.

Dotty Harmer had recovered, and was able to sit up in bed at Lulling Cottage Hospital and receive visitors bearing flowers and little home-made cakes and fruit. Once she had been made to realise that all the animals were being cared for, to the point of cosseting, she had taken a turn for the better. She could not get over Harold's kindness and was delighted to think that her father's sledge had proved so useful.

'I always say,' she told her visitors, more times than they cared to count, 'that it is wise to keep *everything*! There's always a time when one finds a use for things. Father's sledge is a case in point.' To be proved right did more to help Dotty's progress than all the pills which she was persuaded to swallow.

Betty Bell came to see her as soon as the weather released her from her distant cottage, and she resumed work at Dotty's and Harold's again. Another released prisoner was Nelly Tilling who went back to 'The Drover's Arms' as soon as possible, and flung herself, with joyful abandon, into scrubbing the traces of the weather from the brick floor in the bar. It was the reward of her zealous labours which was to give Albert Piggott the greatest moment of his life.

Nelly set out to see how he had fared during the snow-storm, with a basket on her arm. She carried it carefully, through the darkening afternoon, and looked forward to making a pot of tea for herself and Albert when she reached Thrush Green. It was wet and muddy along the field path past Dotty's cottage and her shoes were soon soaking. She was glad to reach the shelter of Albert's kitchen and take them off. Albert seemed almost pleased to see her, and the kettle was already humming on the hob.

They exchanged news of the storm. Albert described the horrors of the mess he had had to clear up in the church, the ordeals he had undergone to get the coke free from snow and the difficulty he had found in keeping the larder even moderately filled.

Nelly countered with her own privations and – a sly stroke – how much she had worried on Albert's account.

'There I was,' she told him, rolling her dark eyes at him, 'wondering how you was managing without someone to cook you a bite or clean the place up. Kept me awake at nights, it did, hoping you was looking after yourself.'

Albert appeared a little touched by her solicitude, and gave a kindly grunt as she poured his tea.

'I brought something for you to have a look at,' she went on. 'Mrs Allen give it to me for doing a bit extra. It's a little clock she bought cheap, but it won't go. You mended my mother's wrist watch a rare treat, and you might be able to see to this. It's real pretty.'

She fished in the basket at her feet and produced a newspaper parcel. Albert undid it gingerly and set a little gilt clock on the kitchen table.

'I've seen one like this afore,' said Albert ruminatively. 'Can't think where for the minute.' He turned the pretty thing about in his horny hands.

'It's French,' he said, still musing.

'Mrs Allen bought it off Bella Curdle, you know, Sam's wife—' began Nelly conversationally, but was cut short by a thump of Albert's fist on the kitchen table which made the tea-cups rattle.

'That's it!' cried Albert. 'This is Miss Watson's clock, I'll wager.'

'Never!' gasped Nelly. 'Are you trying to tell me that this is the clock that got stolen? And that Sam was the chap as done it?'

'That's right!' chortled Albert gleefully. 'That's it!'

'But why should Bella sell it if she knew Sam had pinched it? It'd be bound to be found out.'

'Don't suppose Sam told Bella,' pointed out Albert. 'And I bet Bella never told Sam she'd sold it to Mrs Allen. How did it happen, anyway?'

Nelly said that Mrs Allen had told her that Bella was worried because she was behind with her payments for the clothing club. The young woman occasionally helped to dress poultry or do piece-work on the farm and was a frequent visitor to 'The Drover's Arms.' She had brought the clock one day to Bessie Allen and asked her if she would give her a pound for it. Although Bessie did not want it, she had taken pity on the feckless Bella and had given her a pound and kept the clock. Later, touched by Nelly's arduous efforts after the snow, and knowing that she admired the gilt clock, she had made her a present of it.

'Well, it's Miss Watson's by rights,' insisted Albert. 'Give it here, my gal, and I'll walk along and show her. She'll know well enough.'

'Wait for me,' said Nelly, drawing on her wet shoes again. 'I'll come with you.'

This seemed an admirable opportunity to consolidate her position with the headmistress. For who knew, thought Nelly, shrugging on her coat, how soon she might be living at Thrush Green, conveniently placed to take over the cleaning of the village school?

Unaware of the visitors who were about to descend upon her, Miss Watson sat before her fire pondering upon a most upsetting incident. A pile of history test papers lay on the hearth-rug, a red pencil across the top, but Miss Watson could not bring herself to begin marking.

It had happened only an hour or two before, as the children were dressing to go home. The two little Curdle girls were struggling into their coats when their father appeared. He had the van outside, he said, and as the lane was still awash with melted snow he thought he would pick them up as he was passing.

Miss Watson rarely saw Sam. Occasionally Bella met the children, trailing the toddler behind her, but Sam seldom showed his face at the school. He seemed a little disconcerted to see Miss Watson in the cloakroom. Normally Miss Fogerty saw the children off, but today she had left early to keep an appointment with the local dentist.

He bent down to help his younger daughter tie her shoelace. Something in his movements gave Miss Watson a shock. A moment later she had a second shock. Unable to feel the laces properly with his gloves on, Sam had tossed them on the floor beside the child's feet. Miss Watson had seen those gloves before. They were knitted grey ones, bound with leather and they had gripped a heavy stick.

Miss Watson had felt so sick and so faint that she had been unable to speak. Sam had departed with his offspring, wishing her good afternoon civilly. Since then her mind had been in turmoil.

Should she ring the police on this shred of evidence? Was it, in fact, evidence? There must be thousands of pairs of gloves like that. But she was sure that she had recognised Sam as he had bent suddenly in the cloakroom. Was she justified in confiding her suspicions to the police? If only dear Agnes were here, how helpful she could be!

As her agitated thoughts coursed through her throbbing head the bell rang at the front door, and she went to answer it.

'Why, come in, Mr Piggott,' she cried. 'What brings you here?'

That evening a police car splashed along the watery lane to Nod and Nidden and stopped outside Sam Curdle's caravan.

The next morning Sam appeared before the magistrates and was told that he would be called before Quarter Sessions at the county town to answer his serious charge.

That same day Albert Piggott was treated to so many pints by the regular customers at 'The Two Pheasants' that he fell asleep in the stoke-hole of St Andrew's at half-past two and did not wake until the great clock above him struck five. It was as well, he thought muzzily, as he stumbled homeward, that Nelly Tilling was spending the day at her sister's.

If Nathaniel Patten's memorial were to be erected in time for his birthday on the fifteenth of March, then haste was needed, said Edward Young, who had been in communication with the young sculptor whom he much admired.

Consequently, a meeting was called of Thrush Green Entertainments Committee, when the design was to be approved and the sculptor definitely commissioned.

The meeting was to have been held, as usual, in the village school, but the tortoise stove had developed a mysterious crack which let out fumes and smoke in the most unpleasant manner. Miss Watson, in some perturbation, had mentioned this to Harold Shoosmith when he called to return three balls, a rubber quoit and a gym shoe which had landed in his garden.

'We'll have it at my house,' he said, with secret relief, for the thought of being wedged into the infants' desks for an hour and a half on a bleak January evening had cast its shadow before. 'There's plenty of room, and I'll send a message round.'

He rang the rector last of all.

'Come and have supper here first,' he said. 'The meeting's not until 8.15, and as far as I can see there will only be about half a dozen of us.'

The rector was delighted to accept. Mrs Butler had just told him that she thought there would be enough of yesterday's corned beef hash left for his evening meal, and he had been resigned to his lot. Although he was not a greedy man, the thought of good food and good company greatly cheered him.

He arrived at a quarter past seven and the two men had a splendid steak and kidney casserole and apple tart which Betty Bell had come back specially to cook. The rector thought wistfully how competently Harold managed his domestic affairs, and remembered his own meagre fare and dismal surroundings which he seemed unable to alter.

'Do you know anything about this young man of Edward's?' enquired Charles Henstock later, as they toasted their toes and waited for the rest of the committee members. 'You know, I'm devoted to Edward, and have the greatest admiration for his work – they tell me he has a wonderful flair for domestic detail in his housing plans. But, just occasionally, I wonder if he is not a trifle too advanced in his ideas for the rest of us. Those walls of his – all different colours – and that pebble dash square he has let into his doorstep 'for excitement of texture,' I think it was, seem a little out of this world sometimes. The Thrush Green world, I mean. I suppose we're rather stick-in-the-mud, but we really don't want a jagged piece of metal that looks like a heron with the stomach-ache put up for ever on the green, do we?'

'We certainly don't,' said Harold forcibly. 'But I don't think you need to worry. After all, it's for that very purpose that the committee is meeting tonight. To protect Thrush Green from dyspeptic herons, or – worse still – a bunch of bladders of lard in stone all lumped together and called "Bounty," is *exactly* what we're here for, my dear Charles.'

The rector appeared somewhat comforted and sipped his excellent coffee.

'I must confess,' he said, expanding under the influence of shared confidences, 'that I am relieved that Ella wasn't asked to tackle the job. She is a most gifted person, believe me, *most* gifted. But I find that strong rugged effect in her work a little overpowering. I fear I'm still at the stage of admiring flowered chair covers, and liking water-colours on the wall.'

'And what's wrong with that?' responded Harold sturdily. 'But I agree with you that Ella's well out of it. She would have "had a bash," as she so elegantly put it, I feel positive. She's a brave woman and I can quite see why Dimity relies upon her.'

The rector looked up quickly.

'I sometimes think it is the other way round,' he said. 'Beneath that timid manner of Dimity's there's a very strong and fine character. For all that Ella bullies her – or appears to – I think she feels a deep affection for Dimity, and takes more notice of her gentle suggestions than we realise.'

'You're probably right,' agreed Harold. 'You're a better judge of character than I am.'

'I've known them both for many years now,' replied the rector. 'I have the greatest respect for them,' he added, with a careful preciseness which reminded Harold of one of Jane Austen's heroes.

'I gather it's reciprocated,' commented Harold drily, 'even if Ella doesn't go to church more than twice a year.'

'One can't expect everyone to be as devoted as Dimity,' answered the rector reasonably.

'She's as devoted to you as she is to the church,' said Harold quietly, and watched his friend's face grow pink and decidedly alarmed.

'I think you do her a wrong there,' said the rector hesitantly. 'She is a deeply religious woman and would attend services whoever might be in charge.'

'I've no doubt about that,' said Harold, rising to his feet to make up the fire. 'But she also finds pleasure in your company.'

He pointed a log at the perturbed rector and waggled it for emphasis.

'You underestimate your charms, Charles, as I've told you before.'

The rector was saved from answering by a thunderous knocking at the front door. They heard Betty Bell hurrying from the washing-up to answer it, and the sound of a booming voice which set the dinner gong vibrating.

'Ella,' said Harold. One did not need to live long at Thrush Green before recognising that voice.

Ella and Dimity entered, closely followed by Edward Young and Doctor Bailey. The rector greeted them with his usual warmth, hiding his inner agitation with considerable success.

'There are only the six of us,' said Harold. 'Shall we stay by the fire?'

There was a chorus of assent.

'Though that question does remind me of Violet Anderson's last dinner party,' said Ella, 'when she cut a veal pie and said: "I do so hope you like veal" and we all meekly muttered "Yes." As a matter of fact, I very nearly said: "No, I loathe it; so count me out and I'll have a banana," but I bit it back.'

'Good manners frequently drive one to dishonesty,' agreed the rector. 'It's a nice point to consider – whether one should offend one's host or one's conscience.'

Edward Young took out an enormous envelope and began to undo it rather fussily.

'Perhaps it would be as well to look at the designs at once,' he began, a little pompously.

'I'll read the minutes, and apologies, if I may,' replied the rector mildly, and the younger man bowed his head curtly. As an ambitious man, fast climbing his professional tree, he was beginning to be a little impatient of such petty matters as the minutes of Thrush Green committees.

The rector dispatched the usual business competently, and then looked towards the envelope.

'We're all looking forward to seeing the designs,' he said. 'I take it that the young man is really interested?'

'Oh, very, very,' answered Edward, tugging at the envelope. 'He is an interesting fellow and has just finished some outstanding murals for a new nursery school.'

'Oh, how sweet,' cried Dimity. 'What about? Animals and things?'

'I shouldn't think so,' said Edward, looking as shocked as if Dimity had made an improper suggestion. 'He's very mature in his approach, for his age, and he realises that young children see through the façade of accepted nursery illustration to the elemental truths.'

'Oh, for pity's sake,' implored Ella, 'stop talking like a second-rate psychologist and let's see what the chap's done! You're putting us off before we start.'

Edward had the grace to turn pink, realising that the rest of his hearers silently agreed with Ella's forthright plea.

'I made him understand,' he went on, 'that we preferred a traditional bronze figure as near to a photographic resemblance as he could manage. He found the pictures that you sent of great help, sir,' he added, with unusual deference, to Harold.

'Good,' said Harold. 'You seem to have handled it admirably.'

'Well you certainly didn't think we'd stand for a great lump, reeling and writhing and fainting in coils, with holes in its middle, did you?' demanded Ella, still belligerent.

For answer Edward handed her a large sheet of paper and she was momentarily silenced. He passed others to the rest of the gathering and they studied the plans with interest.

Harold saw, with overwhelming relief, that the suggested design was reassuringly life-like. The young man proposed to show Nathaniel in a typical pose, either reading from a book or studying a plan for one of his own mission schools. If the picture were anything to go by, he had exactly caught the chubby amiability of the frock-coated missionary and made an attractive job of it.

'What exactly is an elevation?' asked Dimity.

'What are the arrows for?' asked Ella.

'Is this a different suggestion?' queried the rector.

Edward patiently answered all the questions that were fired at him. There were several designs, each slightly differing in stance and size, but all acceptable to the committee.

Finally they decided upon the one which Harold had liked, and then the important question was asked.

'Can he get it done in time?' asked Harold.

'He says he can,' said Edward. 'He's absolutely free at the moment and he works at white-heat once he starts.'

'More than the local builders will,' commented Ella. 'I suppose they'll be doing the plinth to this young man's design. I bet he's ready first.'

'We haven't settled that incidentally,' replied Edward. 'He gives three suggestions here, if you notice. They're all quite low, to suit the character of the green.'

'Quite right,' said the rector. 'One doesn't fancy a Nelson's column or even a stone armchair perched up by the chestnut trees on Thrush Green. This looks most suitable.'

'Three steps up,' commented Ella, 'and in York stone. Very nice too. Rather like George Washington who used to stand on the grass outside the National Gallery. Still does, for all I know.'

'One can't help feeling it was a trifle tactless of the Americans to present us with a reminder of the general who overcame us,' observed the rector thoughtfully. 'But on the other hand I think we showed exemplary civility in accepting it and giving it such a place of honour in our capital city.'

'A case of no offence meant and none taken, let's say,' said Harold, with a smile. He handed back the papers to Edward Young, who was busily making notes for the sculptor's reference.

'I think we all agree that a bronze statue, in position four, is the best choice?' he asked, looking round the company.

'With plinth number one,' cried Edward, still scribbling rapidly. 'If I may say so, I think you've made an excellent choice, and I can assure you that the work will be first-class. I'll tell him to get on straight away.'

'Please do,' said the rector, 'and tell him we are delighted with his plans.'

Edward Young suddenly looked a little diffident.

'There is the question of money,' he said. 'The materials will be expensive, as you know. I wonder if it would be possible to advance something to this young man?'

'I don't get paid till I've finished,' said Ella flatly.

'But he may be very poor,' pointed out Dimity compassionately.

'I think that would be in order,' said the rector, looking across at Harold Shoosmith. 'It is often done, I know, in this sort of matter. Shall we take a vote on it?'

Ella snorted, but raised her hand with the rest.

'Right,' said Harold briskly, 'I'll see to that, if you like, as I'm treasurer, I believe. You'll have to let me know how much, of course. Meanwhile, what about a drink?'

He made for the corner cupboard where he kept his bottles, and the meeting ended to the clinking of glasses and the chatter of six old friends, all well content with the evening's work.

18. Spring Fever

THE day after Dotty Harmer came home from hospital, Ella made her way across Thrush Green, down the little alley between 'The Two Pheasants' and Albert Piggott's cottage, and so reached the footpath that threaded the meadow and finally wound its way to Lulling Woods.

It was one of those clear mild days which come occasionally in mid-winter and lift the spirits with their hint of coming springtime. Catkins were already fluttering on the nut hedge behind Albert's house and the sky was a pale translucent blue, as tender as a thrush's egg-shell.

Two mottled partridges squatted in the grass not far from the pathway, like a pair of fat round bottles. Ella looked upon them with a kindly eye. They mated, she had been told, for life, and though she did not think much of married bliss, yet she approved of constancy.

Her mind turned from the partridges, naturally enough, to the possibility of Dimity marrying. Nothing had been said between the two friends, and Ella often wondered if she had imagined a situation which did not, in fact, exist. But ever since the day when she had faced her own fears she had held fast to her principles. If Dimity chose to leave her, then she must wish her all the happiness in the world and make her going easy for her. It was the least one could do in gratitude for so many years of loyal friendship, and the only basis on which that friendship could continue.

Dotty's door was opened by Betty Bell, who had offered to stay at the cottage until Dotty was fit to live alone again. She still went to work as usual for Harold Shoosmith, for Dotty was quite capable of pottering about and amusing herself, but her friends were relieved to know that Betty slept there and could keep an eye on her eccentric charge.

'Well, tell me all the news,' said Dotty, when Mrs Curdle had been scooped off the armchair and Ella settled in it. 'What's been happening at Thrush Green?'

'You've heard about Sam Curdle, I suppose?' asked Ella. 'He's coming up at the Quarter Sessions next month – and it's a funny thing, Dotty, but it seems that he might have been your egg-thief too.'

'Really?' said Dotty agog. 'Oh, how I wish I'd caught him in father's man trap! No one would have felt in the least sorry if I'd caught Sam Curdle, even if his leg had been broken.'

'A peculiarly unchristian attitude,' pronounced Ella, taking out her shabby tobacco tin in order to roll a cigarette. 'It seems that Paul Young and that fat friend of his – Christopher Someone – have had a hidey-hole in one of Harold Shoosmith's trees, and they saw Sam go to your hen house one afternoon.'

'There!' said Dotty, slapping her thin thigh which was covered by a brown hand-woven skirt. 'What did I tell you? If I'd had my man trap we'd have had this all cleared up months ago.'

She pounced on another aspect of Ella's account.

'But what were the children doing in Harold Shoosmith's garden? Surely they knew they were trespassing? Children seem to have no idea of the difference between right and wrong these days. Not enough caning, my father always said – and he was invariably right. I was caned every Saturday night when I had my hair washed,' added Dotty, with some pride.

'What on earth for?' asked Ella, astonished.

'I screamed, dear. Screamed and screamed, and my father thought it unnecessary.'

'But if you were caned,' persisted Ella, shocked at the thought, 'you probably screamed more.'

'Oh, I did indeed!' Dotty assured her blandly, 'but I think

my father felt that I then had something to scream for. It gave him some comfort, I feel sure.'

Ella drew in a large breath of rank smoke and blew it forcefully down her nostrils. Mrs Curdle, who had been hanging about on the hearthrug waiting her chance to get back on the chair, departed in high dudgeon to the kitchen, her tail erect.

'Harold Shoosmith knew they used the tree as a meeting place,' said Ella, 'but he didn't mind. It gave them a lot of innocent fun, he said, and they did no harm.'

Dotty grunted with disgust at such softness.

'Come to that,' continued Ella, taking up the cudgels on Harold's behalf, 'you'd have looked pretty silly if those boys hadn't been trespassing and heard your bell.'

Dotty had the grace to admit it.

'I've sent Mr Shoosmith,' she said conspiratorially, 'half a dozen bottles of last season's home-made wine – all different. Betty Bell took them up this morning and she says he was quite overcome.'

And well he might be, thought Ella grimly. She had sampled Dotty's wine as well as her other concoctions, and knew, to her cost, that the local ailment called 'Dotty's Collywobbles' could be appallingly painful. She made a mental note to warn Harold against sampling his present.

She smoked in silence, while Dotty rattled on, delighted to have someone to talk to.

'I can never thank him enough,' said Dotty warmly. 'So very kind, so attentive – Thrush Green is all the nicer now that he lives here. Does Dimity still see a lot of him?'

The question startled Ella.

'As a matter of fact, they're out together now,' said Ella. 'Otherwise Dim would have come with me. Field Club again, you know. They've gone to see some prehistoric barrows in

Bedfordshire, I think. Unless it was Berkshire,' added Ella, who had never been geographically inclined.

'I really think something might come of it,' said Dotty calmly. She picked up a piece of grey knitting from the floor by her chair and began to busy herself with it. Even Ella realised that she had turned the work the wrong way round and was knitting the second half of the row on top of the first half. It accounted, Ella supposed, for the peculiar shape of the garment and for the alarming number of holes. But she was too perturbed by Dotty's last remark to point out her knitting errors.

'Dimity and Harold, d'you mean?' asked Ella gently, all her old fears returning.

'Yes, dear,' said Dotty, needles clashing. 'Most people seem to think there might be a match. I hope so. But what will you do?'

'I think we'd better wait and see,' said Ella, feeling that everything was going rather too fast for her comfort. 'Dimity's never said a word to me, and Harold is charming to everyone he meets, as you know. If I were you I'd scotch these rumours, not spread them.'

'There! And now you're cross,' exclaimed Dotty. 'Well, don't say I didn't warn you. When something's happening right under your nose it's often difficult to see it. But the outsider, you know—'

'Oh, fiddlesticks, Dot!' burst out Ella exasperatedly. 'You're imagining things!'

'We'll see! We'll see!' chanted Dotty, nodding her grey head and squinting at her crazy knitting. She looked more like a witch than ever.

Ella felt she could bear no more. She rose clumsily to her feet, smote her old friend on the back in a comradely manner, and made for the door.

'I'll come again, Dotty, but I must get back now. Take care of yourself, and don't get any more queer ideas in your head.'

She boomed her good-byes to Betty Bell and let herself out into the welcome fresh air.

Sometimes old Dotty made you feel as loopy as she was herself, she thought glumly, as she stumped back along the footpath. But the maddening thing was that the wretched creature was so often right!

With the departure of the snow and a spell of milder weather, preparations began on the site of Nathaniel's statue. A small area was roped off, and a tarpaulin shed housed three cheerful workmen who brewed tea, and sometimes worked, during the short winter day.

The concrete mixer drowned poor Miss Fogerty's voice in the infants' room and she became adept at miming her instructions to her admiring class. Games in the playground received the children's divided attention, as their eyes were directed far more often to the activity on the green than to that on their own territory. Staunch devotee of Nathaniel Patten as Miss Fogerty was, at times she wished him further.

The progress of the work gave the inhabitants of Thrush Green a new interest. Now that something was really happening even the lukewarm members of the community were stirred with anticipation. The butcher from Lulling and his followers, who had aired their protests at Christmas-time, made no further trouble, presumably washing their hands of the whole affair. But Harold and the rector were still worried about the person who should be invited to unveil the memorial. Time was getting short, and since the failure of their mission in Pembrokeshire they had racked their brains to think of someone suitable for the great occasion.

'You'll probably have to do it yourself,' said Harold to the rector.

'Indeed, no!' protested Charles Henstock. 'It would be most unsuitable. We really must try and think of someone – preferably someone connected with the mission station itself, I think.'

'But they'll all be at the jollifications there,' pointed out Harold. 'I told you they were getting ready for the most terrific celebrations before I left.'

The rector sighed gustily.

'I shall go for a long walk this evening,' he said, at last. 'Very often things are made plain to me on a solitary walk. I may perhaps think of something.'

'Let's hope it works tonight,' commented Harold. 'We're running things a bit fine, if you ask me.'

Whether the long solitary walk had anything to do with it, or whether the rector, in his parish visiting, had met infection, no one could say; but before the week was out the good man was in bed at the rectory with a high temperature and the most fearsome headache.

Mrs Butler supplied a light diet of lemon water and dry biscuits, arriving at the bedside in a state of exhaustion after each trip upstairs, and with a martyred expression which caused the rector added misery, as indeed it was intended to do.

He had been ill for two days before Harold Shoosmith heard of it, and he went straight over to see his friend. What he saw appalled him. A small oil stove was the only means of heating the lofty room, and this was not only quite inadequate but revoltingly smelly.

'Have you called the doctor?' asked Harold, troubled by the apparent weakness of his friend.

'Oh dear no!' exclaimed the rector. 'He is far too busy with people who are really ill, and Mrs Butler is looking after me very well.'

'I think you should see him,' said Harold. 'This room's far too cold, and I'm sure you should be having more nourishment than those biscuits.'

'I haven't much appetite,' the rector said weakly. 'And I don't feel like troubling Mrs Butler for dishes that might be difficult to cook.'

'A boiled egg and some warm milk shouldn't strain her resources,' commented Harold tartly. 'Could you manage that?'

'I really believe I could now,' confessed the rector. 'I must be over the worst.'

Harold made his way downstairs and gave firm orders to Mrs Butler.

'I'll take it up myself,' he said, with authority. 'He needs careful nursing, I can see. And I shall take it upon myself to give Doctor Lovell a ring.'

It said much for Harold's manner that Mrs Butler complied with his request swiftly and also with willingness.

'He's not too bad,' Doctor Lovell said to Harold, after he had inspected the patient. They were alone downstairs in the rector's chilly sitting-room.

'I think it's that she-dragon of a housekeeper that's at the bottom of this,' continued Doctor Lovell in a cheerful shout which must have been easily heard in the kitchen. 'I've told her to light a fire in his bedroom and to keep the whole house warm. It's a dismal hole, isn't it?'

'I agree,' said Harold. 'Something will have to be done about Mrs Butler. She simply takes advantage of Henstock's good nature.'

'She's pretty tied, at the moment,' said the young doctor thoughtfully. 'It might be a good idea to let her have the afternoons off, let's say, and she might do her stuff more willingly then while the rector's ill. She makes him worse by going into the room with a face like a thunder cloud.'

'That could be easily done,' said Harold. 'I'll come in myself, and I've no doubt other friends will take a turn.'

And so it fell out that for the next ten days, whilst the rector kept to his bedroom and marvelled at the sight of a real fire in that long-cold grate, Harold or Dimity and Ella took it in turns to spend the afternoon at the rectory in order to relieve Mrs Butler.

Charles Henstock found it delightful to settle down to his afternoon sleep with the distant murmur of friends' voices and movements downstairs to keep him company. Somehow the house was alive again, as it had been in his dear wife's time. He had been lonely so long that he had almost forgotten the security and comfort of a shared home. When he awoke, after his brief nap, it warmed his heart to think of the tea party which would take place in his room, and he looked forward to the tinkling of the tea tray advancing up the stairs bearing, more often than not, some particularly attractive morsel cooked by Ella or Dimity.

'I really feel so much better,' said the rector to Harold one afternoon. 'Lovell says I may get up tomorrow. I asked him if I'd be fit to go to the Diocesan Conference next week, but he says he'd rather I didn't.'

He sighed sadly, and pushed a printed sheet towards Harold across the counterpane.

'Two or three excellent speakers, you see. I'd like to have heard this young bishop from West Africa particularly.'

'But I know him!' exclaimed Harold, putting down his tea-cup hastily. 'The mission station's in his diocese. How long's he staying in England, I wonder?'

'Why?' asked the rector, surprised at his friend's excitement.

'Don't you see? He's the very chap to unveil the memorial! What could be more fortunate?'

The rector's chubby face grew pink with pleasure.

'What an excellent idea! Now, how can we find out? Could you telephone to our own bishop, do you think, and find out more about it?'

'Certainly I will,' said Harold, bolting down a large mouthful of Dimity's sponge-cake. 'I'll do it at once.'

He paused at the door, doubts suddenly assailing him.

'He's a terrific admirer of Nathaniel's,' he added. 'I hope to goodness he's not made plans to celebrate the anniversary at his mission station.'

'I don't think he will have done, somehow,' answered the rector simply. 'I've a feeling this is a direct answer to prayer.'

It certainly looked like it, thought Harold ten minutes later, as he returned up the stairs. The young bishop, he had been informed, was in England for a three months' study course at Oxford. He had been given his address and telephone number, and he waved the paper triumphantly as he entered the bedroom.

'We'll call an emergency meeting of Thrush Green Entertainments Committee,' he said joyfully, 'and see the reaction.'

'We couldn't do better,' answered his friend, with quiet conviction.

19. Albert Piggott is Won

FEBRUARY lived up to its name of 'Fill-Dyke.' The month began with a succession of rainy days, and people began to fear that the end of the winter would be as uncomfortably wet as its early months had been.

Miss Watson and Miss Fogerty looked at the muddy brick floor of the cloakroom at the village school and shook their heads sadly. Their little brood had just rushed homewards through the rain, mad with joy at being released.

'One really can't blame them,' commented Miss Watson, listening to the diminishing screams and shouts as the children tore away. 'They've missed their playtime all this week. And doesn't the school look like it!'

'Mrs Cooke will put it straight,' comforted Miss Fogerty.

'That's just what she won't do!' responded Miss Watson energetically. 'At least, not for long. Look what the child brought this afternoon.'

She handed over a crumpled and grubby note, written apparently on the fly leaf torn from a cheap paper-back novel. It said:

Dear Miss

Shall be late up scool today as doctor wants to see me as baby cumin whitzun will tell you what he say tonite

Yours

Mrs Cooke

'Well!' said Miss Fogerty flabbergasted. 'Would you believe it?'

'Easily,' said Miss Watson flatly. 'And this won't be the last. The problem is, what to do about a reliable caretaker.'

'There's that fat woman,' ventured Miss Fogerty. 'She seems very willing, and I believe she's a wonderful worker.'

'I've been thinking of her myself,' confessed Miss Watson, 'during recitation lesson. We could ask her to take over temporarily from Mrs Cooke and see how things work out.'

'Much the best thing,' agreed Miss Fogerty, in a businesslike way. It was still delightful, she found, to be consulted as an equal in school affairs. Sam Curdle, wicked though he was, had inadvertently brought happiness to Miss Fogerty on that wild distant night.

'Come and have tea with me, Agnes dear,' said her head-mistress, 'and you can help me compose a letter to Mrs Tilling.'

Much gratified, the little assistant followed her headmistress across the playground to the schoolhouse.

The result was that four days later, with the letter safely stowed in her bag, Nelly cast a triumphant eye over her new territory as she was shown round the school by Miss Watson in the evening. Her heart leapt as she saw the well-stocked cleaning cupboard with its new scrubbing brushes, tins of scouring powder, long bars of neatly stacked yellow soap, and brooms, brushes and dusters in dazzling variety. Her spirits quickened at the sight of the muddy floors, the finger-marked paintwork, the dull brass handles on the scratched cupboards, and the windows so hoary with dirt that some bold, and unobserved, imp had drawn a figure upon one of them and labelled it 'TECHAR' with a mischievous finger. Here indeed was scope for her powers, thought Nelly exultantly!

'The post would certainly be yours for some months,' explained Miss Watson, 'and I think it might well prove permanent, as Mrs Cooke feels that with another baby to think of it might be better to find work nearer her home. It is quite a step here for her.'

'Poor thing,' sympathised Nelly, drawing a finger along a hot-water pipe and surveying the collected dust with much concern, 'she must have been finding it too much for some time.'

'I gather that she might be offered a job at the farm where her husband works,' continued Miss Watson, thinking it best to ignore Nelly's opening. Village schoolmistresses are adept at such strategies. 'She should know very soon, and then we could tell you more. You may find, of course,' continued Miss Watson, 'that you don't like the job here, or that the journey is too far. It's quite a long way from Lulling Woods, particularly in weather like this.'

She gazed through the school window at the drizzle veiling Thrush Green.

'I'll manage,' Nelly assured her robustly. If she played her cards right, she told herself privately, she wouldn't be tramping from Lulling Woods much longer. As for the work, her hands itched to get at it. 'I'll be here at half-past four next Monday,' promised Nelly, 'and make a start.'

She must break the news to Bessie and Ted Allen she told herself as she wished Miss Watson good-bye in the school porch; but meanwhile there was a more important campaign at hand.

Hitching her bag over her arm, Nelly Tilling set out in search of Albert Piggott.

She found him in his kitchen, immersed in the newspaper spread out before him on the table. The odour of fried bacon surrounded him, and a dirty plate and cutlery, pushed to the corner of the table, showed that Albert had just finished his evening meal.

He grunted by way of greeting as the fat widow dumped herself down on the other chair, but did not raise his eyes from his reading.

'It says 'ere,' said Albert, 'that that fellow as robbed the bank yesterday got away with twenty thousand.' His voice held grudging admiration.

'I just been up the school,' answered Nelly, undoing her coat.

'Oh ah?' said Albert, without interest. 'This chap knocked three o' the bank fellows clean to the floor, it says. Alone! Knocked three down, alone!'

'I can 'ave that job if I want it,' said Nelly. 'I've said I'll start Monday. It's a good wage too.'

' "He told our reporter," ' read Albert laboriously, ' "that he was lying in a wolter of blood." Think of that!' said Albert ghoulishly. ' "A wolter of blood." ' He began to pick a back tooth with a black finger-nail, his eyes still fixed upon the print.

'It'll be quite a step every day from Lulling Woods,' went on Nelly, delicately approaching her objective. 'I'm supposed to go in first thing in the mornings too, to light the stoves and dust round.'

'Oh ah?' repeated Albert absently. He withdrew a wet

forefinger from his mouth and replaced it damply on a line of print. ' "He was detained in hospital with a suspected skull fracture and injuries to the right eye." '

'I wish you'd listen,' said Nelly, exasperation giving an edge to her tones. 'I got something to tell you.'

Albert stopped reading aloud, but his eyes continued to follow his moving forefinger.

'Don't you think the time's come, Albert,' wheedled Nelly, 'when we thought of setting up here together? I mean, we've known each other since we was girl and boy, and we seem to hit it all right, don't we?'

A close observer might have noticed a slight stiffening of Albert's back, but otherwise he gave no sign of hearing. Only his finger moved a little more slowly along the line.

'You've said yourself,' continued Nelly, in cooing tones, 'how nice I cook, and keep the house to rights. You've been alone too long, Albert. What you wants is a bit of home comfort. What about it?'

A slight flush had crept over Albert's unlovely countenance, but still his eyes remained lowered.

' "It is feared," ' Albert read, in an embarrassed mutter, ' "that 'is brain 'as suffered damage." '

'And so will yours, my boy!' Nelly burst out, rising swiftly. She lifted Albert's arms from the table, sat herself promptly down on the newspaper in front of Albert and let his arms fall on each side of her. She put one plump hand under his bristly chin and turned his face up to confront her.

'Now then,' said Nelly, giving him a dark melting glance. 'What about it?'

'What about what?' asked Albert weakly. It was quite apparent that he knew he was a doomed man. At last he was cornered, at last he was caught, but still he struggled feebly.

'You heard what I said,' murmured Nelly seductively,

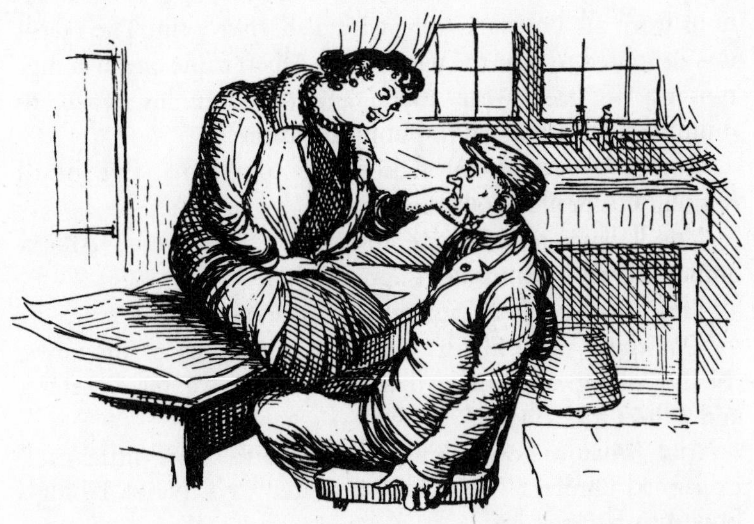

patting his cheek. 'Now I've got the job here, it'd all fit in so nice.'

Albert gazed at her mutely. His eyes were slightly glazed, but there was a certain softening around his drooping mouth.

'You'd have a clean warm house to live in,' went on his temptress, 'and a good hot meal midday, and all your washin' done.'

Albert's eyes brightened a little, but he still said nothing. Nelly put her head provocatively on one side.

'And me here for company, Albert,' she continued, a little breathlessly. Could it be that Albert's eyes dulled a little? She put her plump arms round his shoulders and gazed at him closely.

'Wouldn't you like a good wife?' asked Nelly beseechingly.

Albert gave a great gusty sigh – a farewell, half-sad and half-glad, to all his lonely years – and capitulated.

'All right,' said he. 'But get orf the paper, gal!'

* * *

By the end of the week Albert was accepting congratulations from all Thrush Green, with a sheepish grin. The rector was delighted to hear the news when Albert came one evening, twisting his greasy cap round and round in his hands, to mumble that he wanted to put up the banns.

'You're a very lucky fellow,' he told him. 'I've heard nothing but praise about the lady.'

'You'll have to find one for yourself,' answered Albert, emboldened by his master's approbation.

'I really think I shall,' agreed the rector, smiling.

'One thing,' said Ella to Dimity when she heard the news, 'Nelly Tilling will make that cottage smell a bit sweeter – and Albert too, I hope.'

'And what a good thing for Piggott's poor little cat!' exclaimed Dimity. 'It was such a waif always. Nelly Tilling's bound to fatten it up.'

'Isn't it fortunate?' said Miss Watson to Miss Fogerty. 'To think that she thought of settling in Thrush Green so soon after getting the job!'

'She may, perhaps, have thought of it before,' pointed out Miss Fogerty, with unusual perception.

'Molly Piggott – I mean Curdle – will be pleased,' said Joan Young to her husband Edward. 'It means she won't have to worry too much about the old man while she's so far away.'

'If you ask me,' said Ted Allen to his wife Bessie, sad at the loss of such a good worker at 'The Drover's Arms,' 'she's plain barmy to marry that man!'

'Ah!' breathed Bessie, 'there's no gainsaying Love. Hearts rule heads every time!' She had always been romantic from a girl.

As the month wore on the weather improved, and tempers with it. The workmen, who had been unable to do much in the rain, now returned much refreshed from their rest, and the base of Nathaniel's statue was fast nearing completion. Edward Young brought glowing reports of the progress of the young sculptor and it really seemed as if Thrush Green would be punctual for once and have everything in apple-pie order for the missionary's anniversary on March the fifteenth.

The mild weather allowed the schoolchildren to play outside, much to their teachers' relief. The new school cleaner, whose doughty right arm had scrubbed and polished with considerable effect, also welcomed the dry spell, and the good people of Thrush Green, so long winter-bound, pottered about their gardens, admiring the silver and gold of snowdrops and aconites, and watching the daffodils push their buds above ground.

One sunny afternoon, Ruth Lovell wheeled her infant daughter's pram along the road to Thrush Green. It was wonderful to feel a warm breeze lifting one's hair, and to feel light and strong again. Ruth's spirits rose as she saw the buds on the lilac bushes as fat and plump as green peas. On the other side of the road some willow bushes grew beside a shallow ditch. Already, Ruth could see, the brown buds were showing a fringe of silvery fur, soon to turn to yellow fluff, honey-scented and droning with bees.

But it was the great sticky buds of the horse-chestnut trees which formed the avenue outside her old home on Thrush Green that caused Ruth's heart to stir most strongly. She looked with affection at the sight which had given her joy all her life.

She paused under the trees, her sleeping baby before her, and let her eyes rest upon the familiar scene. On her right, behind the white palings, the children were at play, their distant voices competing with a blackbird's as he trilled and whistled from the Baileys' gate-post on her left. Above her stretched the strong interlacing branches of the chestnut avenue, and higher still a blue and white sky of infinite freshness.

Before her lay the thick green sward upon which her own daughter would be crawling before the summer ended, and there, some fifty yards away, the workmen clanged their tools and whistled, preparing for the great day.

Soon, thought Ruth, joyfully, it would be spring-time again, a time of hope and new life. Before long Mrs Curdle's fair would be assembled on Thrush Green again, and though the old lady would no longer dominate her little world, yet her spirit must surely be with Ben and the great-grandson she had never seen as the fair filled Thrush Green with music and fun on the first day of May.

As she watched the bright scene before her she heard the clang of a distant gate, and saw Ella's sturdy figure emerge from her garden and set off across the green, past St Andrew's, to the alley-way which led to Dotty Harmer's. She was swinging a basket merrily and did not see the motionless figure under the chestnut trees.

'Egg-day!' thought Ruth to herself, and rejoiced at the pleasantness of country life which was so familiar and intimate. 'She'll probably have tea with Dotty, and take great care in choosing her food!'

She watched Ella with affection as she stumped out of sight between 'The Two Pheasants' and Albert's cottage. Unconsciously echoing Mrs Curdle's words on her last visit to Thrush Green, she addressed her sleeping daughter.

'I always feel better for seeing Thrush Green.'

She sighed happily, thinking of the comfort it had brought her through many weeks of misery. It had never failed her. No matter how sore her wounds, the balm of Thrush Green had always soothed them.

She began to push the pram slowly along beneath the trees, over the road which was bumpy with massive roots just below the chequered shade on its surface. As she arrived at Joan's gate she took one last look at the spring sunshine on the green, and caught sight of the rector in the distance.

He was walking purposefully towards Ella and Dimity's house, and in his hand was a large bunch of flowers.

20. Coming Home

THE rector, as he had intended, found Dimity alone at the house, for he too had observed Ella striding towards Lulling Woods, basket in hand, and had remembered that this was the day on which the eggs were collected.

'Why, Charles!' cried Dimity. 'How lovely to see you! I didn't know you were allowed out yet.'

'This is my first walk,' admitted the rector. 'But I wanted to come and thank you properly for all that you have done.' How convenient, at times, thought the rector, was the English use of the second person plural!

'Ella's out, I'm afraid,' said Dimity, leading the way to the sitting-room. 'But I don't think she'll be very long.'

The rector felt a little inner agitation at this news, but did his best to look disappointed at Ella's temporary absence. He handed Dimity the flowers with a smile and a small bow.

'Freesias!' breathed Dimity with rapture, thinking how dreadfully extravagant dear Charles had been, and yet how delicious it was to have such treasures brought to her. 'How very, very kind, Charles. They are easily our favourite flowers.'

The rector murmured politely while Dimity unwrapped them. Their fragrance mingled with the faint smell of wood smoke that lingered in the room and the rector thought, yet again, how warm and full of life this small room was. Ella's book lay face downward on the arm of a chair, her spectacles lodged across it. Dimity's knitting had been hastily put aside when she answered the door, and decorated a low table near the fire. The clock ticked merrily, the fire whispered and crackled, the cat purred upon the window-sill, sitting four-square and smug after its midday meal.

A feeling of great peace descended upon the rector despite the preoccupations of the errand in hand. Could he ever hope, he wondered, to have such comfort in his own home?

'Do sit down,' said Dimity, 'while I arrange these.'

'I'll come with you,' said Charles, with a glance at the clock. Ella must have reached Dotty's by now.

He followed Dimity into the small kitchen which smelt deliciously of gingerbread.

'There!' gasped Dimity, 'I'd forgotten my cakes in the excitement.'

She put down the flowers and opened the oven door.

'Could you pass that skewer, Charles?' she asked, intent on the oven's contents. Obediently, the rector passed it over.

'Harold is coming to tea tomorrow,' said Dimity, 'and he adores gingerbread.' She poked busily at the concoctions, withdrew the tins from the oven and put them on the scrubbed wooden table to cool.

The rector leant against the dresser and watched her as she fetched vases and arranged the freesias. His intentions were clear enough in his own mind, but it was decidedly difficult to make a beginning, particularly when Dimity was so busy.

'I must show you our broad beans,' chattered Dimity, quite unconscious of the turmoil in her old friend's heart. 'They are quite three inches high. Harold gave us some wonderful stuff to keep the slugs off.'

Fond as the rector was of Harold Shoosmith, he found himself disliking his intrusion into the present conversation. Also the subject of slugs, he felt, was not one which made an easy stepping-stone to such delicate matters as he himself had in mind. The kitchen clock reminded him sharply of the passage of time, and urgency lent cunning to the rector's stratagems.

'I should love to see them sometime,' said Charles, 'but I wonder if I might sit down for a little? My legs are uncommonly feeble after this flu.'

Dimity was smitten with remorse.

'You poor dear! How thoughtless of me, Charles! Let's take the freesias into the sitting-room and you must have a rest.'

She fluttered ahead, pouring out a little flow of sympathy and self-reproach which fell like music upon the rector's ears.

'Have a cushion behind your head,' said Dimity, when the rector had lowered himself into an armchair. She plumped it up with her thin hands and held it out invitingly. The rector began to feel quite guilty, and refused it firmly.

'Harold says it's the final refinement of relaxation,' said Dimity, and noticed a wince of pain pass over the rector's cherubic face. 'Oh dear, I'm sure you're over-tired! You really shouldn't have ventured so far,' she protested.

'Dimity,' said Charles, taking a deep breath. 'I want to ask you something. Something very important.'

'Yes, Charles?' said Dimity, picking up her knitting busily, and starting to count stitches with her forefinger. The rector, having made a beginning, stuck to his guns manfully.

'Dimity,' he said gently, 'I have a proposal to make.'

Dimity's thin finger continued to gallop along the needle and she frowned with concentration. Inexorably, the little clock on the mantelpiece ticked the precious minutes away. At length she reached the end of the stitches and looked with bright interest at her companion.

'Who from?' she asked briskly. 'The Mothers' Union?'

'*No!*' said the rector, fortissimo. '*Not from the Mothers' Union!*' His voice dropped suddenly. 'The proposal, Dimity, is from me.' And, without more ado, the rector began.

'Oh Charles,' quavered Dimity, when he had ended. Her eyes were full of tears.

'You need not answer now,' said the rector gently, holding one of the thin hands in his own two plump ones. 'But do you think you ever could?'

'Oh Charles,' repeated Dimity, with a huge happy sigh. 'Oh, yes, please!'

When Ella came in, exactly three minutes later, she found them standing on the hearthrug, hand in hand. Before they had time to say a word, she had rushed across the room, enveloped Dimity in a bear-hug and kissed her soundly on each cheek.

'Oh Dimity,' said Ella, from her heart, 'I'm so happy!'

'Dash it all, Ella,' protested Charles, 'that's just what *we* were going to say!'

Harold Shoosmith heard the good news from the rector himself, that same evening, and was overjoyed.

'I can't begin to tell you how pleased I am,' he said delightedly, thumping his friend quite painfully in his excitement. 'And now you can get rid of that wretched Mrs Butler.'

'Upon my soul!' exclaimed the rector, his smile vanishing, 'I had quite forgotten all about her. What a dreadful thing!'

'Think nothing of it,' Harold assured him. 'She'll be snapped up in no time by some other poor devil in need of a housekeeper.'

He took a letter from his pocket.

'By the way, I've heard from the bishop.'

'Ours?' asked Charles.

'No – theirs. He says he'll be delighted to unveil the memorial.'

The rector's face glowed happily.

'Isn't that wonderful? I'm most grateful to you, Harold, for arranging all this. Without you Thrush Green would never have remembered Nathaniel at all, I fear.'

'I suggest the bishop stays here overnight,' said Harold, 'and I'll get Betty Bell to cook for a small supper party. Ella and Dimity, of course, and one or two more who would like to meet him.'

'Thank you,' said the rector, 'that would be very kind.' He looked across the green towards Dimity's house. 'It will be a great pleasure to be able to entertain again. The house has been so cheerless I haven't liked to invite anyone to stay. I'm afraid Ella will miss Dimity very much.'

He looked with a speculative eye at his companion.

'I suppose you don't feel towards Ella—' he began.

'Charles, please!' protested Harold faintly, closing his eyes.

Thrush Green wholeheartedly rejoiced in the news of the engagement. The rector's sad plight had been a source of great pity, and Dimity, for all her timid and old-maidish ways, was recognised as a woman of fine character and sweet disposition. Some said that Ella had 'put upon' Miss Dimity too long, and not a few hoped that Ella would regret her past bullyings, and realise that she was at fault.

In actual fact, Ella's spirits were high. Now that the blow had fallen she found that the changed circumstances invigorated her. That Dimity should have chosen the rector still surprised her, for although in the last week or two she had suspected that the rector's feelings were warmer than before, yet she had for so long envisaged Harold Shoosmith as the only real claimant of Dimity's affections that it was difficult to dismiss him from her conjectures.

Within a week of the announcement Ella had decided to move her workbench from the kitchen to the sitting-room and to have a cupboard fitted on the landing for her painting materials. Dimity was equally engrossed in planning her new abode.

The wedding was to take place quietly in the summer, and meanwhile the rectory was to be completely refurbished and decorated as Dimity thought best. It gave the two friends a common interest, and lessened the inevitable pangs of parting after so many years, as they threw themselves wholeheartedly into their preparations.

'It was good while it lasted, Dim,' said Ella philosophically one evening, as they packed some china to be taken across to the rectory. She was thinking of the little house which they had shared.

'It will go on lasting, Ella,' said Dimity. But she was thinking of the friendship which they had shared.

As the fifteenth of March drew near, the inhabitants of Thrush Green turned their attention to the approaching ceremony. The workmen had finished their task in good time, and three fine steps of York stone formed a pleasant cream-coloured plinth for the statue which was due to arrive at any moment.

'The only thing that worries me,' confessed Harold to Charles, 'is whether it will be worth looking at. It would be dreadful to find it looked all wrong on the green after so much effort.'

'The thing that worries me,' answered the rector, 'is finding the rest of the money.'

'But you know—' began Harold, and was cut short.

'Yes, I do know. You're much too generous. But at the moment the fund is only just over a hundred pounds, and I shudder to think of the final cost.'

Harold Shoosmith put his hand on his friend's shoulder.

'Don't you realise that this is the culmination of almost a lifetime's ambitions?' said Harold, with conviction. 'I've dreamt about this for years. Nathaniel Patten meant a great deal to me when I was in Africa. His life and work brought me to Thrush Green – and I hope I'll never leave it. Don't rob me of a very real pleasure, Charles. This statue may be Thrush Green's memorial, but it's also a thank offering on my part for hope when I needed it abroad, and happiness at finding myself in Nathaniel's birthplace.'

'I understand,' said Charles Henstock. 'And thank you.'

The statue arrived two days before it was to be unveiled. It was a perfect spring day, warm and sunny, with a great blue and white sky against which the black rooks wheeled and cawed. In the gardens of Thrush Green the velvety polyanthus was in bloom, and a few crocuses spread their yellow and purple petals to disclose dusty orange stamens.

A little knot of people gathered round the lorry to watch the sacking wrappings being removed from the swathed figure. The young sculptor watched anxiously as his masterpiece emerged. He was a well-dressed thickset young man, red of face and bright of eye, and a source of some amazement to various Thrush Green folk who had been expecting someone looking much more pallid and artistic with, possibly, a beard, a beret and sandals.

He helped his workmen hoist the bronze figure upright on the grass and seemed pleased to hear the little cries of pleasure which greeted the life-size figure. It was indeed a fine piece of work. He had caught exactly the benevolent facial expression and the Pickwickian figure in its cut-away coat. There was something lovable and friendly about its size and its stance, and Thrush Green prepared to welcome Nathaniel warmly.

It took several hours to put the bronze figure securely upon its plinth and by that time all Thrush Green had called to see its new arrival.

'Do you think it should be covered?' asked the rector anxiously of the artist.

'I don't think we need to worry,' smiled the young man. 'He's going to stand on Thrush Green in all weathers for many years, I hope.'

Very early, on the morning of March the fifteenth, before anyone was astir, Harold Shoosmith leant from his bedroom window and looked upon the fulfilment of his dreams. Later in the day, the unveiling would take place, and there would be speeches, cheers and crowds. But now, in the silence of dawn he and his old friend were alone together. Exactly one hundred years ago, on just such a March morning, Nathaniel had been born in a nearby cottage.

A warm finger of sunlight crept across the dewy grass. At last, thought Harold, the long winter at Thrush Green had ended and, exiles no longer, both he and Nathaniel Patten were home again.